"Do you have any enemies?"

Bryn closed her eyes. "No."

"The killer's treating you differently than the other victims. He never threatened them." Or had they not confided in anyone? No, they were too smart to hide that. But Bryn hadn't called the police.

He looked at her then as she neared the road, silhouetted by the headlights that came into view. It was the first car he'd seen since their walk in her neighborhood. In the darkness its headlights blinded him. Eric raised his arm over his brows. "What in the world...?"

But it was too late.

The engine roared and the truck barreled straight for Bryn, who stood frozen in the street.

"Bryn!" He sprinted toward her, threw his arms around her and hurled them into a ditch just as the truck disappeared around the corner.

He felt her breath against his cheek but he didn't move. "You okay?"

She nodded. "You?"

Then it hit him and fear rumbled through him. "He knows where you live...and he'll be back."

Jessica R. Patch lives in the mid-South, where she pens inspirational contemporary romance and romantic suspense novels. When she's not hunched over her laptop or going on adventurous trips with willing friends in the name of research, you can find her watching way too much Netflix with her family and collecting recipes to amazing dishes she'll probably never cook. To learn more about Jessica, please visit her at jessicarpatch.com.

Books by Jessica R. Patch

Love Inspired Suspense

Fatal Reunion
Protective Duty

PROTECTIVE DUTY

JESSICA R. PATCH

HARLEQUIN® LOVE INSPIRED® SUSPENSE

Recycling programs
for this product may
not exist in your area.

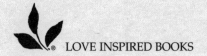 LOVE INSPIRED BOOKS

ISBN-13: 978-0-373-44751-0

Protective Duty

I know what I'm doing. I have it all planned out—
plans to take care of you, not abandon you,
plans to give you the future you hope for.
—*Jeremiah* 29:11

For Bailey. I marvel at your strength, courage and determination to accomplish anything you set your heart on.

Thanks go out to

My agent, Rachel Kent, for always being in my corner and believing in my writing.

My editor, Shana Asaro.
Thank you for your keen eye and amazing editorial skills.

Incredible critique partners: April Gardner, Jill Kemerer, Michelle Massaro and Susan Tuttle.

Huge thanks to "Mr. Anonymous"
for taking time to help me with the law enforcement information. If something's *not* right, it's on me!

And to Jesus. For Your glory always. I adore You.

ONE

Bryn Eastman refused to think about the bullet that had pierced her abdomen. She would not fixate on how her attacker's gloved hands had wrapped around her throat or how she'd let down her guard and almost died a year ago.

Her nerves pulsed anyway as she slid into her FBI windbreaker. Her first case since the shooting.

Slivers of October moonlight snaked between the autumn leaves. Yellow crime scene tape beckoned her toward the grove of towering trees. Blue lights slashed the dark as flashlight beams swiveled across the ground. Camera crew vans lined the parking lot, morbidly eager for a story.

Special Agent in Charge Towerman had brought Bryn up to speed CliffsNotes-style. She hadn't been back in Memphis long enough for the detailed version. Tonight's victim made number four. She'd been left in Overton Park for families, children—the world—to view. An ache thumped in Bryn's gut and spread into her chest.

She stared at the frenzy.

Would the lead homicide detective welcome FBI assistance? Welcome a female's assistance? Experience told her he wouldn't, but she hoped so anyway. This was a man's world she maneuvered through. And while there were many who accepted her as an equal, there were just as many more who didn't think a woman had any business in law enforcement.

She'd spent almost a decade validating that she was able, strong and brave.

Until Ohio had shaken her to the core.

This string of murders had Memphis, and the mayor, in a panic. Victimology was Bryn's expertise. So here she was, even though SAC Towerman had been reluctant to send her in.

She needed this chance to confirm that she was still capable. Still brave. Still strong. Bryn yearned to bring justice for the victims whose lives had been tragically taken, and she needed to be in the field to accomplish that.

The question was, could she rise above the jitters and insecurity and give the grieving families her very best? She owed it to them. And she needed to prove herself to SAC Towerman. Then she could stay in the field, not chained to the desk where he'd planted her the minute she stepped foot in the Memphis field office.

She locked her car, squared her shoulders and strode across the parking lot toward the crime scene. Pausing as she neared the tape blocking civilians and the news crew, she swallowed a hard lump in her throat and stifled the eerie sensation of being watched.

This wasn't Cleveland.

Showing her creds to the uniformed officer, she slipped under the crime scene tape, ignoring the caterwauls of the news crew begging for information. FBI on the scene had their mouths salivating and their heads spinning.

Did they even know this latest victim was the morning talk show host for *Wake-Up Memphis*? She strode toward the tree line. The crime unit was in place. A man dressed in jeans and a fitted black leather jacket accenting his broad shoulders—his hair as dark as the jacket—stood near a woman examining the body. She hadn't admired a man in a long time. Shouldn't be admiring one now, but he was hard not to notice.

A stocky older man with gray hair stepped from the shadows. Pug nose and potbelly. He held up his badge. Deputy chief of investigative services. "Agent Eastman?"

"That's me." She smiled and corralled her flimsy windbreaker. "We appreciate you calling us in. Whatever we can do to help, we will."

He extended his hand, and she shook it. "We're glad to have you. Your reputation precedes you. I'll be honest, I didn't expect you to be so young."

She was only twenty-eight, but some days Bryn felt ancient. "I'm up to the task." She had to be. Lives depended on her. No room for failure.

"I believe you, and we're ready to work in tandem. Let us know what you need." No indication he was blowing smoke. But it wasn't the chief she had to work with directly. It was the lead detective who she now suspected might be the man in the leather jacket—the man whose hair and physique caught her eye and quickened her pulse.

The deputy chief motioned for her to follow him. *Yep. Guy in the leather.*

"Special Agent Eastman, meet Detective Eric Hale. He's the lead on the case."

A needle ripped across one of the many records in her memory. She'd packed that name away. Okay, maybe not packed it away, but she'd definitely not played it on the turntable of her mind in a while. Not since they'd been a serious couple nearly a decade ago. The song was too haunting.

He turned around and she could finally see his face. Time had been good to him. His boyish appearance was masked by a couple of days' worth of dark scruff gracing his chin and cheeks. It suited him. Appealed more than she'd ever admit. Bryn's heart skittered.

Guess he hadn't played her record in a while, either.

His eyes were wide and swirling with questions. Bryn had prayed they wouldn't ever meet again; the pain would be unbearable. Even now she felt the punch, knocking the breath from her. Those prayers, like so many before, had fallen on deaf ears. She'd given up on prayer. Given up on faith. On God. He'd taken too much from her.

She thrust her clammy hand out, hoping for an air of confidence and that Eric wouldn't refuse it and humiliate her in front of her peers. It wasn't his style, but he'd have every right to.

Her older brother *had* murdered his sister, Abby, seven years ago.

Eric glanced at her hand and slowly clasped it. Firm but not crushing. Still warm and encompassing. Her throat dried out. She'd missed his touch.

"Fancy meeting you here." His eyebrows quirked. Humorous as always, but underneath the light tone he'd tried to pull off, Bryn registered confusion. A truckload of shock. When she'd left Memphis—and him—she'd been on the women's swim team at Rhodes College thanks to a scholarship. No intentions of ever becoming a cop—like Eric.

But then Abby died, and the world changed. Bryn changed.

She cleared her parched throat and assessed the scene, struggling to find her voice. "Not sure *fancy* is the right word. But here I am."

"How?" He scratched the back of his head. "I thought… Weren't you… Didn't you… I mean, *when*?" His brow wrinkled.

"We'll get to all that," she whispered, wishing things didn't have to be so complicated and confusing. "For now, you mind filling me in?" Bryn studied the woman lying atop gnarly tree roots that rose from the sparse grass, fully clothed with hair still damp and clumped to her cheeks.

She never got used to this. Hoped she would never become hardened like some agents.

Eric pointed to the victim. "Bridgette Danforth, cohost of the *Wake-Up Memphis* morning talk show. She appears to have been drowned like the other three women before her. All high profile. The medical examiner will know more when we release the body. A jogger found her. He's over there if you want to question him. I already have but…"

But was she going to take over his case? Trust him or not? That was the rest of his sentence. "Not right now, no." She did want to poke around on her own. Besides, she needed the air. Time to process that Eric Hale was about to be her new partner in a sense. Time to escape the enticing masculine smell of soap, cologne and leather that messed with her head.

"But you *will* want to." His clipped statement said it all. He had no forgiveness, and the fact she was here to try to solve a case he couldn't only furthered his irritation. *Super*.

"I will. And I'll need everything you've got on the previous victims. You can send it over to the FO. I'll review them in the morning." She'd rather work at the field office. Her turf. New, but still.

His nostrils flared, and he clenched his jaw before he saluted. "Yes, ma'am."

She ignored his sour jab, switched on her flashlight and stalked across the park. The wind bucked up, whistling through the trees. Crescent moon. Eerily quiet. Her feet sank in the soft ground. The smell of winter coming sooner rather than later enveloped her. She shone the light, hunting for anything that might have been left behind. A fairly clean park. Not much litter. A few cigarette butts. She edged toward a hedge of bushes that opened into a dense wooded area. Secluded. Interesting that he placed the victim in a more open area and not here, hidden from the parking lot and nighttime joggers. He *wanted* her found, and he was willing to risk being seen. Brazen…or stupid. *No.* Not stupid or he'd have been caught by now.

Something nestled near the tree line. A scarf? Might be the victim's or the killer's. She bent over and caught a whiff of cheap, heavy cologne and cigarette smoke.

Hair spiked on her neck.

From behind, an arm coiled around her neck in a python-like grip. He yanked her against him, pulling her farther into the remote wooded area.

She grabbed for her sidearm, but he was quicker and snatched it from the holster.

"Ah, ah, ah," he growled as his wiry beard scraped against her ear.

Would he shoot her? Shudders rolled down her back as the scene from Ohio chiseled back into her bones. *No.* He couldn't be crazy enough to squeeze off a round. Every officer on the scene would come running. They may not be able to see out here, but they'd hear gunfire.

He tossed her Glock several feet away.

"Who do you think you are? Miss High and Mighty-FBI." His breath smelled of smoke, beer and mints that hadn't done their job. "You got no business here."

Bryn's heart kicked into a sprint.

Fear slicked down her back in arctic streams; a wave of hysteria clouded her brain, stopped her from reacting.

Spots dotted her vision.

"You better back off before you find yourself dead like those other ones."

No.

That's why she was here. For the other ones. To fight for them.

Adrenaline raced, and Bryn rammed her elbow into rock-solid abs. He barely flinched but tightened his grip, and a tattoo covering his hand came into view.

Fight. She had to fight.

She brought her foot down on his. He didn't budge. She glanced down. Boots. Probably steel-toed.

Her attacker dragged her even farther into the woods as he assaulted her ears with vile, hateful words.

"Agent Eastman! Bryn! Hey…you! I'm not sure how to address you these days." Beams of light pulsed in their direction. "Where are you? Marco!"

Eric.

If she could manage a sound, she'd call out to him. She dropped her legs like deadweight, refusing to make this easy for the brute.

Bryn's eyes burned. She needed more oxygen. With this grip, a whimper wouldn't make it from her lips. She sank her teeth into the bionic man's arm. His heavy coat would probably protect his arm from the bite. But she'd try. By granny, if she had to break every tooth out of her gums she would.

"That's your cue to holler back 'Polo.' Bryn? You out here? I'll even take an 'over here.'"

The savage grabbed her hair, which hung in a low ponytail. "This ain't over."

She rammed his rib cage again, but he thrust her in the air and into the cluster of bushes he'd been dragging her away from. Her head popped against the ground with a thud, and white-hot pain seared up her back. Boots pounding and rustling bushes sounded in the distance. He was getting away. Whoever *he* was. Had he been out here all along, hidden away watching from a distance? Was he the killer? She clawed breath into her lungs. Sweet, wonderful breath. Her throat ached, and pain continued to streak down her spine into her tailbone.

"Over…over here," she croaked.

Eric had needed a minute. He still needed a minute. How was Bryn Eastman back in Memphis? And not just back but an FBI agent? He had five billion questions and no time to ask even one.

Fancy meeting you here.

Seriously? That's what came from his mouth the second he laid eyes on her? He'd rehearsed time and again what he'd say if they ever met again. That line had never made it into the script. He flashed his light, hunting for her through the foliage.

"Eastman!" His voice echoed through the silent park. A secluded place to dump a body or attack someone—like Bryn.

Bryn Eastman. FBI. Eric gave his head a good shake. Chief had said the female agent being sent to assist specialized in victimology and profiling, and had an impressive track record for such a young agent. She'd worked on the Dayton Date Rapist case, the Cleveland Creeper case, a few others in Iowa, plus one in New York.

All successes.

But *his* Bryn Eastman?

Whoa. Where had that come from? She wasn't even close to being his. Hadn't been his since their relationship tanked when she was still in college and he was working as a patrol officer. When her brother had turned out to be a serial killer who had set his sights on Eric's sister, Abby.

Which was why they could never be together again.

But that fact hadn't stopped his heart from slamming into his rib cage when she cast those blue eyes on him. Long golden hair secured at her neck. Creamy skin and high cheekbones. She was the epitome of the All American Dream Girl. A California dime—if she were from Cali and not Memphis. Either way she was still a ten.

Where was she? Was she ignoring his calls on purpose?

"Bryn?" Cold pinpricks traveled up his spine. Why wouldn't she call out? About twenty feet ahead, a flock of blackbirds burst from half-naked maples. He cast his light in the direction.

Was that a figure?

His gut tightened. His pulse galloped. *God, please let her be okay.*

"Over...over here."

Eric sprinted toward the sound of her garbled voice and found her slumped against a tree, her hand on her temple. "Bryn!" He knelt. "What happened?" Her bottom lip quivered, and her eyes appeared glassy. "Bryn, talk to me."

"That...way. He went that way." She pointed.

He hesitated.

"Go. Don't worry about me."

How could he not with her face paler than snow and trembling hands? A mix of fear and utter rage pulsed through Eric's veins. Someone had laid a hand on her. Hurt her. God had protected her, though. Two things Eric had never ceased doing: thinking about Bryn and praying for her. Looked like God had been listening.

"Go...you'll lose him."

Eric touched her cheek, then bolted in the direction of the shadow, radioing backup to help canvass the area and letting them know an officer needed medical attention. Weaving between trees, he followed the sound of footsteps that led up a hill and onto the highway.

No one. Where had he disappeared to? He searched the area for a few more minutes. Pulse pounding in his ears, heart hammering, he raced back to Bryn and dropped to his knees at her side. "What happened? Other than you refused medical treatment." First responders were leaving the area.

"I didn't refuse. I politely declined to go to the hospital." She removed her hand from her forehead; a streak of blood trailed down her temple and cheek. "It's a minor abrasion."

It didn't look minor, but there was no point arguing. "The attacker? What happened?" Eric huffed.

"One minute I was picking up a scarf and then out of nowhere…" With shaking hands, she stared at the blood on her fingertips. "I'm… I'm okay, though. I fought." Bryn squeezed her eyes shut, and everything in Eric screamed to gather her close to him, assure her that she was safe. But he couldn't. Instead, he laid a hand on her cheek.

She stood up and winced. "Must have been the killer."

The thought of what could have gone down, and only a few feet away from his protection, was more than he could stomach. Better to make light than fall apart right here and now. "Or someone who really doesn't like you," he teased in a shaky voice.

"Har. Har." She crossed to the left, bent, then retrieved her gun and holstered it.

"He got your gun?" A thump formed behind his right eye. A guy this crazy could have shot her. Killed her!

She nodded. The expression on her face told him to tread lightly, and behind her narrowed eyes pumped raw fear.

"Promise you at least let them check you out before sending them away?" He focused the beam on her injury. "You might have a concussion."

"Eric, I'm okay." She paused, and friendliness coupled with sadness accompanied her half smile. "Thank you, though, for repeatedly asking." She wobbled a bit, and he grabbed her upper arm to help balance her, the nearness overwhelming him. The scent of oranges was dizzying in an oh-so-good way.

"So you think it was the killer? Out here watching?"

"Who else would it be?"

Now that Eric wasn't scared out of his mind, that was a good question. The fact Bryn was back in Memphis where so many tragic things had transpired might mean she was running from something—or someone—in Ohio. "You tell me."

She paused again and peered up at him. Confusion clouded her eyes. "What do you mean?"

"I don't know." He swallowed. "Why are you back? Why here of all places?"

Squinting, she studied him until he wanted to shift his feet. "I know I'm the last person you want to see—"

"I didn't say that." He had mixed emotions about seeing her.

"You didn't have to." She rubbed her temple. "I don't know who it was. I can only assume the killer. I don't have any answers right now. I haven't even had time to look at the case files."

Fine. "He say anything? You get a solid look at him?"

Bryn shook her head. "Got me from behind and put me in an iron headlock. I tried every defense I knew—"

"Even the whistle?" He couldn't help but chuckle. In college, Bryn had carried a shiny silver one on her key ring. Once she'd blown it in his ear. He might have deserved it. She'd always been a hothead. He'd always liked that about her.

She grimaced. "No, not the whistle. Not like I would've had the breath to let out more than a faint tweet."

"I thought you could go like twenty minutes without breathing." Bryn had been a stellar swimmer back in the day.

"Eight, and that's after being pumped with oxygen for thirty minutes and hydrating well. Besides, you can't blow a whistle without air." She tossed him the "duh" look. "Maybe they need to check your head."

He hid his grin. Bryn hadn't lost her feisty tongue. She might not have a concussion after all. "Back to the guy."

"He was tall," she said. "Over six feet. Beard—scraped against my cheek. A fairly full one. Steel-toed boots, so he might be a blue-collar worker. And he had a tribal tattoo on his hand. I think I can draw it."

"Way to observe, Sherlock."

"Thought I was Marco." Her lips twitched. "How about plain old Bryn?"

There was nothing plain about Bryn. Never had been. She stormed up ahead of him, but he spied the tremor in her hand before she shoved it inside her coat pocket.

Eric caught up with her at the crime scene. He put a few techs on the area surrounding Bryn's encounter. Maybe he left a shoe impression. A cigarette butt. An address and phone number tacked to a tree with an arrow.

Bryn picked leaves from her hair and put on a brave front. He'd known her long enough to know when she was hurt. Known her since he and her cousin Holt McKnight were in the Academy together. She was in high school. Too young for him. Until she turned nineteen, and he made his move. Two years together after that, heading straight for the altar and forever. If Rand hadn't heinously intervened.

"What do you have so far?" Bryn asked.

All business. Trying to pretend she hadn't almost been killed with dozens of officers nearby. This guy was either a complete idiot or entirely too confident in himself. Both were dangerous attributes. But he'd run down the trail with her. She might need a few minutes to collect herself. Focusing on the dead victim—not the living one staring straight at him with eyes that had always unraveled him—would help. *God, thank You again for protecting her.*

"I only got here fifteen minutes before you." He stared at the victim. "I'm not a fan of morning TV."

"Because you aren't up." Bryn snorted and shoved her other hand in her windbreaker pocket. "Wind's gonna kill us. We better get while the gettin's good or we could lose evidence."

"Yup." Eric wasn't sure how all this was going to play out. "So, you're assisting? Just assisting?"

Bryn flexed her jaw. "I don't want to take over your

case. I'd like to work together. But if you go getting a chip on your shoulder, I can't promise to play nice. Our past—"

"Won't dictate the case." Eric ground his teeth. Over the years, he'd made peace with what happened. Lots of prayer and extra time in the Word had helped. Some days were harder than others, but he didn't blame Bryn for Rand's actions, and he would work with her to catch the killer. "I've labored for months on this. My partner and me. I want to be the one to get this guy."

"Where is your partner?"

"Honeymoon." *Must be nice.* "Holt never mentioned you'd gone into law enforcement."

"Why would he?"

Why would he indeed? After things crumbled—no, disintegrated—Eric hadn't even mentioned Bryn's name. Not to Holt. "I guess he wouldn't."

"You see him much?"

"Some. He helped out in a case a few months back when he was working undercover to take down a drug dealer who was a suspect in one of our cases."

Bryn raised her chin in a nod. "Here's my card with my email address. I'll make sure a major case room is set aside for us. We can work from there."

Assisting, huh? Felt like taking over. "I'll send the case files tonight and meet you in the morning. You drink coffee?"

Bryn gave a tight-lipped smile. Was she struggling with their nearness as much as he was? Was it regret or resurfaced attraction? Because he was feeling a bit of both. Or maybe she was just loopy from the attack. The one she was shrugging off as if it hadn't happened, which scared him a little.

"Nothing fancy. Just black with a couple creams and a sugar."

She never had been fancy. Didn't need to be. She stood

out without all the bells and whistles. Well, minus the whistle. He chuckled again.

"What?"

"Nothing."

She grunted. "Once we get set up in the room, we'll need to track down Bridgette Danforth's family. Does she have any?"

Eric inhaled the chilly air, struggling to ignore her scent that he'd once loved. "Divorced. No kids. Workaholic."

"How long she been divorced?"

"Few years. You think her ex copycatted the other killer's work?" Eric scratched the back of his head. "The dramatic display of laying her out looks identical to the other three, and we kept that from the public, as well as the fact he takes a token of jewelry. Bridgette is missing an earring."

"Could have come out during the struggle or if he dragged her." She touched her own earlobes. Two simple gold studs in each ear.

"No drag marks. But maybe." Or the killer had taken a trophy like he had with the others.

Bryn scanned the area, ignoring the shouts from the media begging for a statement and asking if she was the new lead on the case. Eric's ears heated. He swallowed his pride. He had to. He needed some assistance.

"I don't want to make any assumptions. Not until I've read the files."

Cautious. That was new. Anything else new? He glanced at her left hand. No ring. His was achingly bare, too. Or maybe she didn't carry the ache of their failed relationship. But then, he knew that wasn't true. The way it had ended between them had affected more than just their hearts. Two families bore the pain.

"I doubt the man who roughed you up was her husband.

Which brings me to the fact we can't ignore." He stressed the word *ignore*. "Did he say anything directly to you?"

Bryn cleared her throat and scuffed her toe along the ground. "Besides some nasty name-calling, apparently, I have no business here, and if I don't watch my back, I might end up like the other four victims."

Why would the killer follow her? If he'd been on the scene watching all along, what made her his focus? Was it chance? She did go off alone. But why come at her? Here? "That makes you a target, Bryn. Where are you staying?" Eric wasn't going to risk this guy attacking her again. He couldn't.

"Holt's letting me shack up in his rental for a while. At least until I can settle in. Why?" Her tone carried wariness.

"Is he staying there with you?"

"No, but I carry a gun, and I know how to use it."

What if the attacker got to her before she could get to her gun…again? Her cousin was a DEA agent, and if he was in between cases Eric had full confidence that Bryn would be safe. Holt was pretty hard-core. "Maybe you should have Holt stay with you."

"Maybe you should get me those case files."

Hardheaded woman. Some things never changed. Not only did he have to worry about solving this case, which had been nagging him for months, but now keeping Bryn safe nipped his heels. "At least let me follow you home. Make sure no one is tailing you."

"'Cause I can't spot a tail?" She glared and whipped her hand into the air, brushing him off.

"Because this guy's no joke. He's gutsy. I don't want him finding you alone again. Do you?"

She raised her chin. Unease darted through her eyes, softening her tough exterior. "I wasn't prepared for that. I am now. I can take care of myself, Eric."

He didn't doubt it. She was strong-minded and strong physically, with a swimmer's body, but Bryn was in danger.

She matched his stare. *Nope.* The woman wasn't going to change her mind. If she wanted to go it alone, fine. He'd tail her without permission. Watch her get inside safely. And pray with extra fervor.

TWO

Sleep hadn't come for Bryn. For those first few moments in the park, she wasn't sure if she was going to live or die. This was the very reason SAC Towerman had requested she see the bureau therapist. She hadn't had time to see one in Ohio because of the quick transfer after her surgery and recovery from the gunshot wound.

But she'd fought last night in the park. Just like in Ohio. And she'd survived.

Only because Eric had shown up. What if he hadn't? She had to believe that she'd have retrieved her complete mental faculties and escaped, taking the attacker down. However, it hadn't stopped every crack and pop in her house from keeping her wide-awake, adrenaline racing until she broke out into a sweat.

The only thing comforting about the night at all was cuddling with her golden retriever pup. She'd stopped by Sport's Authority to purchase a new bathing suit after joining a nearby gym with a pool, and she hadn't been able to resist the puppy. The pet adoption agency had set up in the parking lot, and this fluffy, blond pup had barked his way into her heart.

After consuming half a pot of coffee and walking her new little love, she'd come on in to set up a major case room. Table. Whiteboard. Space to tack maps and charts to the wall. Whatever was necessary to track down this monster, and a monster he was. Bryn had pored over the case files Eric had sent in the middle of the night. Didn't appear his sleeping habits had changed over time. When they'd been a couple, some nights he'd call her as late as two in the morning. Just awake and bored. Although he'd said it was simply because he'd missed her voice, even if they'd been apart for less than three hours, and it had melted her every single time.

Enough trailing down a path of wilted and dried-up rose-petal memories. Back to the case at hand. Bryn sipped her lukewarm coffee and checked her watch—almost 8:00 a.m. In the past five months, four women had been drowned and left in a public park. Bryn had connected the same few dots Eric had. While the women shared similar features, such as thin noses and lips, blond hair and blue eyes, they didn't fit age-wise. The youngest victim was midthirties while the oldest and most recent victim—Bridgette Danforth—had been forty-six. Two were married. Two were divorced. The divorced women had no children. The married women did.

Last night's victim had left her car in the parking lot at the station after the morning taping. Like the other victims, she had seemed to walk away with the killer without a single person noticing. Vanished. Question was, did they know their killer or was he simply a charming man and able to catch his prey off guard, using something to draw their compassion, all the while luring each one into a trap?

The guy who had attacked her held zero charm.

Bryn tapped her pen on the desk and stared at the victim photos she'd tacked to the board. She'd drawn a line to the connections they had, but not a single line joined all four women. What had Eric missed? What was she missing?

"I come bearing coffee." Eric swung into the case room with two cups in hand. So much better than the burned brew she'd been slurping from the bureau pot. He sat it on the conference table near her, his scent revealing a fresh shower and a man who knew how to wear cologne—the expensive kind. But then he had money. A lot of it. Trust-fund cop. Her pulse betrayed her and rode off at a steady gallop. She refused to admire his full lips—extremely kissable lips, surrounded by scruff that concealed two deep-set dimples.

"Thanks." She worked to appear professional, to mask the way his presence did a number on her stomach. Last night, when he'd brushed her cheek and showed concern, it had brought up so many things about him she once loved, including their shared faith. Now hers was shaky at best. Had Eric lost his after what happened to his sister? She wouldn't fault him for it.

This morning, she had to shove the emotions that surfaced back down where they belonged. She didn't have the heart to get rid of them entirely.

He surveyed the room. "You've been busy."

She sipped the fresh coffee, set it aside and eyed him. "You, too. After tailing me home and sitting outside for an hour, you must have been up half the night sending the files over. But you've showered, so I thank you." She mimicked his raised eyebrows. She'd had half a mind to march out there and blow a gasket on him, but civility won out and a tiny sliver of her had been grateful. "I'm not a damsel in distress."

"*Tech*nically…" He cocked his head and grinned.

Bryn held back an eye roll and opened Bridgette Danforth's case file. "We're missing a connection between the victims. I want to go back over the investigation with a fine-tooth comb. Talk to friends and family."

Eric opened his mouth, no doubt to erupt in protest, but Bryn held her hand up. "I trust your work. But I need to step into their lives. I need them to put me in his head. This is how I do my job." Not her favorite part—stepping into a killer's mind—but necessary.

His protest petered out, and his eyes softened. He had the best eyes with long, thick lashes. "I heard through the grapevine you've been very successful. And for being so young."

Young. Old. It was about determination and persever-ance. Passion and motivation. She wanted justice for these victims. For all the victims she championed. She'd always been intrigued by Eric's job as a police officer and Holt's DEA work. But death and evil hadn't been real for her. It was something that happened to other people. Until it raised its ugly head in her own home. She'd been almost twenty-one.

"Just so you know, I've heard good things about you and your work. Me being here isn't about you not being capable."

His eyebrows flashed upward. No, to him it probably felt like a punch to the groin.

"I didn't ask to take over. Okay?"

If Abby hadn't died, they'd likely be married. But then she may not have followed the career path she was on now, and she was supposed to be burying old emotions.

"Okay." Eric cleared his throat. "You really like this job, don't you?"

"I like putting a dent in evil's fender." She rubbed her clammy hands on her pants. "I… I had to do something. I couldn't just hop in a pool and pretend if I kept swimming laps what happened to your family, to mine, wouldn't exist."

"So you moved to Ohio with your parents?"

"After Rand's trial. Yes. We all needed…new." And yet she was back. For another fresh start.

Eric popped the lid off his coffee cup and sipped. "Why did you come back to Memphis?"

She hadn't answered him last night. Wasn't sure she had the answer. And him asking had hurt. Was he sorry she'd come back? How could a place with so many horrifying memories also provide her with some comfort? Familiarity? Or because her best memories—many of them involving Eric—were in Memphis? "Point is I'm here. And we have a job to do. Can we try to set aside the pain and our past? At least to get through this case?" She'd crumble if she didn't build a wall.

Eric's nostrils flared, and he flexed his right hand—a hand that used to stroke her cheek often or meld with her own, fingers laced together. "Compartmentalize. I'm good at that."

Didn't she know it, and he generally used humor to do it. "Okay, I can read the files all day long, but I want to hear about the investigation from you. By the way—" she stole another sip of her brew "—your handwriting is atrocious."

Eric walked to the board. "We got a call on our first victim on a Friday morning back in the beginning of May. Female in a park in Collierville. Thirty-eight. Hair and clothing damp. Turned out to be a professor at Rhodes. Cat Weaver. Married. Daughter in high school."

"Taught sociology."

Eric nodded. "No assault. Just drowning. No drugs in her system, but then we didn't know of anything specific to check. Stomach contents showed it was regular ol' city water she drowned in. Same with the other two and I'll guess same with our newest victim, Bridgette Danforth."

Bryn flipped through reports. "Victim two was found in early July. Victim three in early September, but he broke pattern by striking again now in October instead of next month." Something must have triggered the escalation, giving Towerman and the mayor reason to pull her in so quickly.

The killer's pattern had changed now, making him unpredictable.

"Wish we knew why. There's nothing to indicate they'd been bound. Just walked off willingly with this guy. All cars abandoned, like Bridgette's. We snooped on the husbands and the exes. Didn't find anything. Alibis checked out."

Would any of them have gone willingly with the guy that had assaulted Bryn in the park? Which reminded her. "I drew that tribal tattoo. Had one of our analysts run tattoo recognition software through NCIC and the Department of Homeland Security. Maybe we'll get a match. But I made a copy in case you might have seen it or heard about it when interviewing family and friends."

She showed him the picture and he shook his head. "No, nothing ever mentioned about a tattoo. Man, I'd love a break in this case. Been praying and trusting God every day for one."

Looked as if Eric's faith hadn't been destroyed. She almost asked him how he'd stayed strong. Instead she focused on the case and stared at victim number two's photo. "Tell me more about her."

Eric pointed to her photo on the board. "Kendra Kennick. She worked for a PR firm. Tulley & Comer. They handle everything from campaigns to scandals. She had a few angry letters."

"I read them. Nothing I'd red flag. Steam blowing mostly."

"Still, I chased those leads."

"And?" Bryn cocked an eyebrow.

"Steam blowing." Eric smirked. "She left behind a husband and two children. Eight and five. The mayor jumped in at that point. Family friend. Kendra helped him with his last mayoral campaign."

"Hmm. Was the mayor at Rhodes's fund-raising gala? The one our sociology professor vanished from?"

Eric tipped his head. "He's a piece of work, but I'm not sure he's a serial killer."

Bryn shrugged. "Was he there?"

Eric's neck flushed. "I never checked."

"Check. Can we link him to the other two victims?" Bryn wasn't ruling him out. Darkness often masqueraded as light.

"He knows Bridgette Danforth. He's been a guest on *Wake-Up Memphis*."

Bryn stood and crossed to the board. "And what about victim three, Annalise Hemingway? Can we connect them?"

Eric inhaled. Exhaled. "I wouldn't think directly. She's a divorce attorney and he's still with his wife—"

"But he kept Kendra Kennick, the PR specialist, on retainer. What if she wasn't only helping him with his campaign? What if he had marital issues? Maybe his wife gave Annalise a visit. She does specialize in high-profile divorces. Maybe the threat of Annalise scared him faithful... or more discreet." She only represented wives, which was also interesting. "How long was Annalise divorced? Ten years?"

"Yes. From Alan Markston. He's remarried to a girl fresh out of private-school-plaid skirts and oxford shoes. Like I said, alibi checked out. But I got a gut feeling he was a real tool."

"Lovely." Bryn would like to pay him a visit. "I guess it'd be a dumb question to ask if she had enemies."

"She was the go-to attorney if you wanted to squeeze blood from a turnip out of your not-so-better half." Eric reached into his leather jacket and pulled out a package of Twizzlers. "You want?" He held one out.

Bryn heaved a sigh. "Strawberry?"

"Is there any other flavor?" An incredible, lady-killer grin filled his face.

"Cherry for one." She held her hand up and passed on the chewy strip of licorice.

"Ones that count." He popped the edge in his mouth like

a cigarette and stared at the board. Sweet strawberry flavor wafted into her nostrils.

"Let's swing by and chat with Bridgette's ex-husband and then hit the station and talk to her coworkers. See if we can figure out where she was the night before. Tomorrow or later tonight I can interview past victims' family and friends. And we'll need to cover her condo."

"I already had her cell phone sent in to one of your analysts. They're pulling calls and texts. Her purse and contents are in Evidence."

"If her purse was in her car, then she was likely taken from the station. Security footage?"

"Yeah, wouldn't that be nice. None."

"Thanks. For…being so cooperative. I appreciate it." She tried not to get too lost in those brown eyes.

Eric shifted a shoulder up, chewed, swallowed. "You driving or me?"

"How about you? I need to reacquaint myself with the city." She grabbed her purse, slipped on her knee-length charcoal-gray trench and belted it at the waist. When she glanced up at Eric, he turned away. Had he been checking her out? The thought stirred a flutter in her stomach. The last thing she needed was to feel flutters over Eric Hale.

Eric's throat turned to sawdust. He'd told himself a thousand times he wasn't going to appreciate her femininity. It was all professional. He was going to pretend she was his real partner, Luke—with a scruffy jaw and the annoying habit of popping his knuckles. But when she cinched the belt at her slender waist and her hair fell past her shoulders, the five o'clock shadow disappeared, and he caught himself admiring her. Looked as though she'd caught it, too.

He held the door open, refused to cast his eyes anywhere that would be disrespectful, then wiggled another Twizzler from the package to occupy himself. They ambled down the hall to the elevator. If she'd been offended, she hadn't let on.

Eric rolled his licorice around his lips. "You know if we start digging into the mayor's life, we'll have to be invisible about it."

Bryn punched the elevator button and stared at the steel doors. "Yep."

Maybe he *had* offended her.

They walked through the parking lot to his work Durango. Unsure if she'd appreciate him opening her door or not, he paused near the hood of the vehicle. This was work. He hit the fob key and unlocked the doors, then rounded to the driver's side, feeling like a total schmuck for not being a gentleman.

Bryn climbed inside and strapped on her seat belt. "I can't see any of our victims willingly going with a gruff thug like the one who attacked me. Unless…" Bryn adjusted the radio, and he ignored her music choices. She had eclectic taste. Or at least, she used to. Minus country. How could a native Memphian not have a love and respect for country music?

Eric darted a glance at her. Her thin index finger tapped against a full bottom lip. "Unless?" So far, he'd been impressed with her ability to get up to speed at a rapid rate.

"Unless he was at the scene in disguise. In Cleveland…" Her voice trailed off, and she swallowed, her neck bobbing.

"In Cleveland, what?"

Bryn's face paled, and she gripped the canvas belt of her coat and stared out the window. What had happened? Eric mentally ran down her cases before transferring to Memphis. The Cleveland Creeper was her last. Whatever had happened might be the reason she left Ohio. And it might be the reason she was attacked.

"Many offenders like to come to the scene and watch, even participate."

"So he might not have a beard or tattoo?" Eric jumped off 385 into Collierville. Bridgette Danforth's ex lived out here on a golf course. *Golf.* His stomach soured.

"No, I'm certain the tattoo was real, which is why I think the beard and boots were his style, not disguise, but... I don't know." She shook her head and pinched the bridge of her nose. Was she second-guessing herself? Overthinking? Bringing up Ohio had flustered her. A sheen of sweat beaded around her forehead, and her long lashes fluttered against her skin as she rapidly blinked.

"So, you up for some barbecue later? We gotta eat, and if I remember right you can tear up some ribs."

She frowned, then grinned. "No, you like ribs. I like chicken. You have a terrible memory."

But she'd smiled, and the lines across her forehead had smoothed out. "Maybe it *was* me that liked ribs. Either way, by the time we finish here and the studio downtown, we'll be close to the Rendezvous. And they should be open by then."

"Hmm... I somehow feel set up to satisfy your pork habit."

Technically she had been set up, but not for food. *Note to self: do not bring up Cleveland.* If and when Bryn wanted to tell him what happened and why she transferred, she would. Unless it was the reason she'd been hurt, and if that was the case he'd find out the details on his own. "What can I say...the stomach wants what the stomach wants."

Her cell phone rang, and she snagged it from her coat pocket. "Agent Eastman." She shifted toward the window and lowered her voice. "Yes, I remember. Thank you for calling." She hung up and went to town clutching the belt on her coat again, leaving wrinkles in the fabric.

"So this is me being nosy."

"This is me telling you to mind your own business." She flashed a mock smile and batted her lashes, but distress filled her eyes. How long could he go without pressing her to share what happened in Cleveland? Everything in him wanted to lean over and comfort her, to tell her whatever it was she was safe now. But it wasn't his place anymore, and that bothered him. They were partners only. Not that partners didn't care or worry about each other, but he couldn't see himself reaching over and stroking Luke's hand. *Picture her with scruff.*

Nope. Didn't work. He flashed his badge to the attendant working the booth and entered a gated community set on a golf course. Brick homes with French shutters dotted perfectly manicured lawns. Fall wreaths graced front doors, pots of mums and whatever else those fall flowers were lined sidewalks and weaved between bushes. The kinds of homes and communities Eric had grown up in.

"You still play?"

"Harmonica?" he joked.

Bryn gave him a wooden look. "You know what I'm talking about."

Golf. "Sometimes. But only when I want to."

Eric could have gone pro. Almost had. But he'd attended a Royal Family Kids' Camp sponsored by his church and things changed. Seeing so many abused and neglected children had tugged his heart in ways golf never could. People who hurt children—abused anyone for that matter— deserved justice. So he'd entered the police academy. But Dad and Mom didn't quite understand the concept of God's leading. According to them, life was what people made it. Destiny was acquired by going after dreams and desires without the need for God's plans.

"Good for you, I guess. I always enjoyed watching you play."

He turned and grinned. Sadness mixed with regret. "I always knew you were there for me. No ulterior motives. No pressure if I won or lost."

"Kinda like you attending my swim meets."

This was winding down a serious path. Emotions were surfacing that he couldn't allow. Too much damage had been done when Abby died. "Well, I have to admit, I was mostly there to see you in a swimsuit."

She laughed. "You're such a guy." Bryn had let his remark go, but Eric knew that deep down she didn't believe that for a second. He'd been there to support her because he cared about her. Her drive and passion were contagious. Even now, he felt it in her skills as an agent.

"I'll take that as a compliment."

"Whatever lights your fuse."

"Do you still swim?" Eric weaved through the subdivision. Large sweet gums towered overhead. An array of gold, red and orange leaves swayed with the fall breeze. Not the best day for golfing.

"Yes. As therapy." She frowned at the word *therapy* as if it coated her tongue in acid. "I joined a gym not far from Holt's rental house. Bought a new swimsuit…and a dog." She sighed. "You golf with your partner? Luke?"

"Luke? Golf? Hardly. But if I wanted to suffer some punishment and box, I'd call him first. I play a few games every now and then with my dad."

"Really?" Surprise lit her face.

"He stopped hounding me about getting back into the game when my profession became useful to him."

The air in the SUV grew thick. He hadn't thought his answer through. He'd said he wouldn't bring up the past and then did anyway.

Bryn rubbed her hand against her thigh. "How…how are your parents?"

Eric pulled into a circular drive and cut the engine.

Brave question.

"Our lives were altered forever, Bryn. How do you think they're doing?"

"Just for the record," she said, "our lives were altered, too. We live with the guilt of what Rand did to not just Abby but the three girls he murdered before her. I grew up with him, and I never knew the darkness in him. I feel guilty for that, as well."

Eric clenched his jaw. "I know. Let's just not talk about it right now, okay?"

He'd rather focus on finding the man killing these women than reliving the tragedy in his own life.

THREE

Bryn white-knuckled her steering wheel as she drove to the therapist's downtown office. The stop at the Danforth residence had been a bust. Mr. Danforth was out of town at a conference until next week. The housemaid had been charmed by Eric. He was good at that. Naturally sweet to everyone. He even had the woman promising to make him empanadas next time he swung by. After that, they ran by the station that taped *Wake-Up Memphis*.

Bridgette Danforth's cohost, Anderson Tawdle, was as plastic as they came, and it was clear there was no love lost on his part, but then Bridgette had been trying to get him fired so she could bring in an all-female cast. That gave Anderson motive to kill her but not the other three victims.

Turned out Bridgette had a massage appointment with her lifelong friend, Sandra Logan, who owned an animal clinic in Germantown. Animals happened to be one of Bridgette's many causes. Causes that she promoted with boldness on her TV show, creating many reasons to hate her. She had mail to verify it.

The interviews had taken longer than Bryn expected, so she canceled on lunch. Eric seemed disappointed and pried to find out why she had to leave in the middle of the day.

Seeing Dr. Elliot Warner wasn't anyone's business. She didn't need colleagues thinking she was unstable or incompetent. Even if seeing a therapist was protocol, it was still humiliating, especially since she wasn't either of the two.

Bryn parked in a lot a block down from Dr. Warner's. Downtown could stand to be cleaned up some. There were abandoned warehouses with cracked windows on one side and trendy places to eat on the other. Grabbing her purse, she stepped out of the car and headed toward his office.

Cracks and loose gravel caught the toe of her shoe. She righted herself, crossed the street and inhaled.

By granny, she had this. She'd prove to Dr. Warner that keeping her behind a desk wasn't utilizing her well, that Towerman hadn't made a mistake by sending her into the field. Maybe the city's and the mayor's panic had been to her advantage. She'd keep her fears buried and only give him information on the case, which he already possessed anyway. As the session progressed, he'd see she was on top of everything. And he'd give a glowing recommendation to Towerman.

The semi-decaying brick building held some old charm. She opened the tinted-glass door. Inside, the building transformed from decrepit and broken to fresh and classy.

Violins harmonized to Pachelbel's Canon in D Major and filtered through hidden speakers. The scent of lavender and eucalyptus wafted through the front lobby. Her shoes clicked against polished hardwood flooring as she crossed to the circular mahogany desk to the left of the foyer. Should she wait for a secretary?

She strummed her fingers along the desk, then sank onto the chocolate-colored leather couch while the violins began their crescendo.

Bobbing her knee and flicking her nails, Bryn gnawed the inside corner of her mouth.

A door down the hall squeaked open. Floor joists creaked and squawked, and then a man in his midforties, attractive, smelling like new money, loomed in the door frame leading into the foyer. Thick chestnut hair cut in a trendy style matched the thin lawn of scruff on his face. Warm amber eyes greeted hers. "I'm Dr. Warner."

"Bryn Eastman."

He glanced at his expensive watch and raised an eyebrow. "You're early. Eager to start?"

Eager to get out. Bryn cracked a shaky smile. "Sure."

"Follow me." He led her down the hallway past a men's restroom, then a women's restroom. His office was to the left. He opened an espresso-colored wooden door and slipped inside. Bryn followed.

Set like a formal living room with a large comfy couch and two leather club chairs surrounding a decorative table, his office was masculine and inviting. A large ornate desk rested in front of a built-in fish tank that lined an entire wall. The tank had to hold at least a thousand gallons.

"Have a seat, Agent Eastman."

Bryn settled in a club chair. No lying on the couch for her. Dr. Warner chose the couch, leaning back comfortably, ankle cocked over his knee. Muscular. Probably from tennis or rowing.

Other than the sounds coming from the filter on the fish tank, silence filled the room and dragged. Was she supposed to start? She had nothing to say. "I like your fish tank. Salt water?"

He glanced at the tank. Schools of fish swam in colors ranging from banana yellow, silver, violet and turquoise to an array of multicolored ones. "Fresh actually. Easier to clean."

She admired the coral, the sand, a small elegant ship and a treasure chest in the corner. The bubbling eased her jumbled nerves. Peaceful.

Bryn studied the blur of colorful fish. "They're beautiful. Eye-popping." So many. How did he keep them from overcrowding? That's how she felt. Overcrowded. With being back in Memphis, working on the rental house, the new puppy, this high-profile case and Eric—working with him and old feelings poking at her.

He leaned forward, his elbows on his knees. "They're all male. They tend to have more color than the females."

"Huh. No one fights for alpha status?" She examined the fish as they weaved in and out of each other's way. She fought for it every day, not so much dominance as equal footing. In her line of work, she was the minority.

"I did my research."

Probably did his research on her, as well. She didn't want to talk about herself. "I like the quiet water, too." Bryn leaned back in her chair. "Which ones are your favorites?"

Dr. Warner checked his watch again. "This session is about you. Do you want to talk about you?"

No. Not in the least. "I'm fine."

"Okay."

Time crept along as silence hung.

Uneasiness broke it.

"I can do this job. I know the risks. I knew them when I pursued this career."

"Do you want to talk about why you pursued this career?"

"You already know why. You know everything." As a contracted therapist by the FBI, he was privy to all of her case files, as well as her dossier. He knew what happened in Ohio. What happened on her first night in the field— the attack. It would all be there in black and white. She couldn't hide any of the facts from him. Her feelings were an entirely different matter. "And as you can see, I'm fine."

If she kept repeating that, he wouldn't believe her. He scribbled on his notepad. Was he writing that she was uncooperative? If she wanted her permanent freedom from the desk, she needed to toss him a bone. SAC Towerman had already had a lengthy discussion with her after the attack

in the park. Was she okay? Could she keep up out there?
Blah. Blah. Blah. He needed her out there as much as she
needed to be out there, but she hadn't missed the skepti-
cism in his eyes and hesitation in his voice.

"I was nervous walking on the scene. And I was afraid
when the attacker grabbed me around the neck. Who
wouldn't be?" Being an FBI agent didn't make her superhuman.

Dr. Warner kept writing, then looked at her again.

Bryn held his gaze. "It had nothing to do with what happened in Cleveland. I did my job there. You know that."
But flashbacks and that same fear had resurfaced. To tell
the good doctor that meant to tell him she wasn't healed.

Well, she wasn't. Never would be. She'd thought about
praying but was fairly certain God had stopped listening
to her prayers. He definitely had stopped answering them,
or she and Eric would be together. Happy. With a family.

She pointed to the file in his lap. "Can't you just sign
off on my paperwork and let me do what I do best? I don't
see the need for these appointments."

The giant obstacle between her and the career that com-
pelled her to take risks stared into her eyes. "You don't see
the need in talking to someone about almost being murdered…twice? Or about the past events that drove you to
this line of work?"

"I saw a family therapist at my mom's request after my
brother…" She couldn't even bring herself to go back in
time. It had been excruciating and pointless. "And, yes,
that's why I pursued this career. I can catch this killer. But
I can't do it behind a desk." Time to show him she could
cooperate and be compliable. "Scared or not, we have to
push past the fear for the greater good. Every agent has
some level of fear."

"You think pushing fear aside is dealing with it?" His
voice was low. Calm. Nonjudgmental.

It was the best she had to offer. He made a strong point with the question, though. Eventually, her fears and stress would snap, and she might put herself or others in danger if she slipped. She just wouldn't slip. Wouldn't let "eventually" come.

"You think by keeping silent you'll get clearance from me. I understand that. I see many agents who think the same thing, but it's not true. However, if you want to sit here every Friday for an hour and say nothing or talk about my fish, then we can do that."

If she talked, if she spilled it all, he might think she was weak and unfit. But if she didn't divulge, he'd assume she was burying feelings and a ticking time bomb. She bobbed her knee, debating what to do. "I... I have trouble sleeping sometimes. Right before I doze off, I see Scott Mulhoney's face, and I might have a mild panic attack—but I assure you it's getting better." She'd long stopped calling Mulhoney the Cleveland Creeper and put a name to his face. Made him human. Even if he'd seemed superhuman.

Hopefully, sharing this much was enough to keep her on the case but not enough to make him think she was incompetent or unfit for field duty.

Dr. Warner nodded. "That's normal. I'd be more concerned if you said you were sleeping like a bear in winter." He crossed to his desk and laid the notes on top, picking up a prescription pad. "I can prescribe a mild sedative."

"Sure." Bryn took the prescription and tucked it in her purse. "Dr. Warner?"

"Yes?"

"You've seen the files. You know what he's doing to those women. They deserve justice."

He crossed his arms, muscles pulling the sleeves of his white dress shirt taut. No wedding ring. Quite the catch. She tamped down a laugh as she caught sight of the fish tank. *A catch.* Eric would have loved the joke. But Eric wasn't going to know about these visits.

"I did see them. I can't help you if you don't let me. Understand?"

Bryn nodded. Her time was over, and they'd barely had a conversation. If she kept that up, she'd end up exactly where she didn't want to be. But she didn't want to talk about her feelings. She didn't want to unearth what she'd buried. She didn't want to air her weaknesses and most private thoughts. "I'll do better next week."

"If you need to talk before then, you have my card. After hours, a service will forward your call to me."

"Thanks." Opening the door, she stepped into the hall and turned right. Dr. Warner laid a hand on her shoulder and steered her left.

"Back door for anonymity. No one sees you. You see no one."

She slipped down the back hallway, out a side door and down the street to the parking lot.

She pressed the fob key and unlocked the car. Something white fluttered on her windshield. Restaurant menu? Coupon for a car wash? Maybe a tract explaining the way to salvation and claiming God's love. Bryn hadn't felt God's love in a long time. All she'd felt lately was abandoned, unwanted, uncared for, and she couldn't figure out why.

She grabbed it and started to crumple it in her fist when she noticed the words. She smoothed it open, hairs rising on her neck. A hollow chill whistled through her body. Head buzzing, she read the block-style words.

Miss High and Mighty FBI,
You're dead!

A crack sounded, and a spray of concrete exploded near her feet. She dropped to her knees, using the car to shield herself from the bullet. Fear rocketed into her throat and sent her head into a dizzying spin.

Grabbing for her gun, she aimed it toward a building, but she wasn't sure where the shot had been fired from. Shooting aimlessly wasn't smart. Safety was.

Heart hammering, sweat popped along her upper lip and forehead.

Metal clinked as another bullet connected with the passenger door. Bryn fumbled for the keys she'd dropped when the first shot unloaded on the pavement.

The shooter's position was high. Probably inside one of the abandoned buildings twenty feet away.

Another bullet hit the hood of her car. She bit back a shriek, and with quaking hands opened her car door just enough to slide inside. She worked to get the key in the ignition and crank the engine. Staying low, she gunned it and peeled out of the parking lot as one more bullet connected with the trunk of her car. Was this the same man who had attacked her in the park? He'd used the same words: High and Mighty.

He'd followed her here. How did she miss that? She had to call in backup. Although, the killer was probably long gone by now. Probably took off the second her car squealed from the lot. The law enforcement agent in her screamed to get the crime unit out here, to call Eric. To go straight to the field office with the note and the bullet that was lying on her floorboard.

Then they'd all know she'd been at a psychiatrist's office. But mostly Eric would know. He'd pry into Ohio and discover the truth.

No, she'd definitely turn the bullets and note in, but she wasn't bringing anyone out here.

* * *

Eric's entire afternoon had been a bust. From the interviews he'd accompanied Bryn on to the lack of hits in the tattoo recognition database.

To top that stellar display of uselessness, he had driven to Edgewood Golf Club—Dad's golf club. Nothing like driving out to be surrounded by workaholic, money-hungry, narrow-minded men—one being your own father—just to bring *great news*. Revealing that Bryn Eastman was back in Memphis and working with Eric on this case. Better he'd heard it from Eric than the five o'clock news.

It had gone over like no cake at a six-year-old's birthday party.

"How dare she come back here! To show her face after what her…her brother did to our family."

"Dad, she's an FBI agent and she's successful. She's trying to make up for the past." It wasn't a stretch to make that deduction. Why else would Bryn end a career in professional swimming and diving and her dreams of coaching a girls' swim team? She'd always been a fan of saving the whales or dolphins. She'd studied biology. Major shift to criminal justice.

Dad hadn't cared.

A steely glare had formed in his eyes. "If you even think of dallying with that girl again—who's beneath us to begin with—you won't have a family anymore. Is that what you want, Eric? To hurt your mother all over again by losing a son? You'd kill her if you did that. You know she has a heart condition."

Dad's fist of hate and truth had sucker punched his gut. Mom's heart had always been weak, but after Abby she'd had two stents. Eric was the only child left. Could he do that to her?

His answer had flown off his tongue with record speed. "Dad, that's never going to happen, but I do have to work with her. I thought you should know. I'd never intentionally hurt either one of you." He never had. Intentionally.

Now he was parked on the street in front of Bryn's house, taking her the lunch that had become dinner. What obligation had kept her from eating? What was she keeping from him? It nagged at him. Right along with the fact she had yet to mention her faith, which had once been a huge part of her life. Had Rand robbed her of that, too? Eric's faith had been shaky for a while, as well. He hadn't let it stay that way, though. *Lord, if she hasn't let You heal her completely, please open her heart up to allow it.*

Eric clambered from his car with a bag of food—chicken for her as requested and BBQ ribs for him with sides and rolls. Her car parked in the drive caught his attention. He crossed over and bent at the waist. Was that a bullet hole?

Storming to the front door, his heart suffering from arrhythmia, he pounded. A dog yipped. Bryn's scolding followed.

The door opened. She'd changed into jeans and a T-shirt the color of island waters. A dolphin jumped an ocean wave on its front. "What are you doing here?" She eyed the food sack. "You brought food?"

He ignored the question. "Why do you have a bullet hole in the trunk of your car?" Eric stepped inside. "And why did I not get a phone call?" The scent of vanilla rode over the smell of an older musty home. A candle burned in the corner on a rickety table by the sofa—the source of vanilla.

Bryn groaned. "I haven't been home but long enough to change my clothes. I intended to call you."

After the fact.

That ate at him.

Bryn stood before him, avoiding eye contact. Fidgety. She'd been shaken. "Something happened today."

Eric's temper rose out of fear. "Yes. You were shot at!" She could have died. He pulled his phone from his pocket and glanced at the screen, then held it up for her to see. "No missed calls. No texts."

She grabbed the bag of food and took it to the kitchen. "Calm down. I know that look."

Eric balled his fists and edged up behind her. She turned around and smacked into his chest; a flustered expression filled her face.

"Calm down? You left me with no explanation of where you were going, then you got shot at! And you want me to calm down?"

The dog jumped on Eric's pant legs and barked. He ignored the ball of fluff.

Sighing, she collapsed on a kitchen chair and tented her fingers on the table, her hair draping over her face. "I needed a few minutes to clear my head, and I might have ripped my pant leg diving from the bullets."

Eric steeled his jaw as the image sent a wave of nausea through him.

"I got a letter."

"What kind of letter?" he asked through clenched teeth.

"The kind that didn't need postage or a return address." Bryn grabbed her purse hanging on the chair and handed him a Ziploc bag with a crumpled sheet of copy paper inside. "The short, sweet and to-the-point kind."

"And the gunfire?"

"Happened while I was reading the note. Three shots. One by my feet. The second at the passenger side door. The last on my trunk when I drove away."

Eric needed to sit down, run his hands over Bryn's face and hands and convince himself she was okay. The killer had never left his victims a note or shot at them. Just like making himself known in the park, this was different. "Where was your car?"

"In a parking lot downtown. I was on personal business... an errand."

Eric glanced at her. Straight face. What kind of errand? What kind of *personal* business?

She handed him a pair of latex gloves. He carefully extracted the letter from the plastic bag and read it.

The knot in his gut turned into a glacier, freezing him from head to toe. Blood rushed into his ears. The glacier slowly melted as fury boiled until it broke out into a sweat on the back of his neck.

He had to cool off. Be levelheaded. Carefully, he replaced the note inside the bag.

Bryn twisted her fingers. "Well?"

"*What* parking lot?" He pinned her with a glare.

She shifted in her seat, then handed him another plastic bag from her purse. "I dug the slugs out when I got home."

"Before you called me? You said you only had time to change clothes."

"I needed to get my bearings together. We can get that to ballistics ASAP." Her cheeks had lost their color, and she hadn't stopped tapping her foot against the linoleum.

As frustrated as he was, Eric couldn't let her feel alone, and clearly she was afraid and nervous. Eric grabbed her clammy hands. "It's gonna be okay. I promise." He gave them a gentle squeeze. "Why won't you tell me where you were? We could go check it out or send a unit."

Bryn freed her hands and tucked a strand of hair behind her ear. "Doesn't matter. He entered an abandoned warehouse and probably wore gloves, which means we won't find prints on the note or the casings—if he didn't take them with him."

He hadn't worn gloves the night he strangled her. Of course, that hadn't been calculated and planned like what happened today. Bryn had obviously thought this through, and it was even clearer she didn't want him or anyone else in that parking lot. What was so secretive about it? For now, he'd let it drop because they had a bigger issue to discuss.

"He's following you. You missed it. Or he knew where you would be. Anyone else know where you were today?"

Nostrils flaring, Bryn snatched the evidence bag out of his hand. "My personal business is mine alone."

She avoided the question. That meant someone might know where she'd been. It gnawed at him and then struck a solid blow to his abdomen. What if she'd come back to Memphis *for* someone? Met someone. What if he lived downtown or worked there? How did Eric feel about that?

About as good as he felt about kale.

Why else hide her location? She must think it'd cause a rift in their working or personal relationship—not that they had anything more than a professional relationship, but they weren't fighting. Was that enough to go against protocol, though?

"You need to tell Holt if you haven't already." If Eric couldn't camp on her couch maybe she'd let her cousin.

Bryn tossed her hands in the air. "I knew you'd say something like that. What if it was you? What if you got tossed into the bushes and shot at? Would you ask Holt to spend the night?"

"Well, no, that's weird."

"You're making my point. Would you move out of your house and stay with someone?"

"Probably not." But he was a man. And as a man who wanted to keep all his parts, he kept that last statement in his head where it belonged.

"Double standard. And I hate it!" Bryn slapped the table. The dog jumped into her lap. "He's a good watchdog. He barks at anything and everything. I'm a light sleeper. And I have a gun at my bedside. What more can I do besides go into witness protection?"

"That last question was rhetorical, right?" He massaged the back of his neck. "Okay, I get it. Bryn is a big girl.

Doesn't mean I won't be concerned." The normal amount, of course.

"I'll be extra careful."

"I'll put a few unmarked cars out here at night."

"I'm not gonna say no to that." She shuddered. Not quite the confident crusader she made herself out to be. At least she could give him that. Didn't feel like enough, though.

"So what's the dog's name?"

"Newton."

"Fig?"

"Wayne." Bryn smirked, and her shoulders relaxed.

"You have weird taste in names and celebrities." He leaned in, elbows on his knees. "You okay?"

Her nod didn't convince him. Not at all.

Eric wasn't okay, either.

FOUR

Newton skittered across the floor and scratched at the back door. Eric wasn't getting the location out of Bryn, not even if he took a crowbar and pried her lips open. Easing off that topic—and the topic of staying home alone—he had to focus on the present and discover who was behind this.

"He wants to go out. I'm shocked he hasn't whizzed on the floor." Bryn grabbed a leash from the hook by the kitchen door. "I could use some air. You?"

Eric could use some answers. "Sure. The food will keep."

He followed Bryn out the front door, waited for her to lock it and they headed down the street. The sun had already started its descent, and Bryn shivered. "Should have brought a coat," she said.

He shrugged off his leather jacket and took the leash while Bryn hesitated, then slipped into it. Looked good on her. Too big. But good.

She half smiled. "Thanks. It's warm."

"Yeah, that's what anger will do to leather."

"You're mad at me?" They walked at an easy pace while Newton sniffed around mailboxes and grass.

Eric sighed. "Well, yeah. You're keeping secrets, ignoring protocol and shutting me out. We're partners for now, at the very least. And partners owe each other honesty."

Bryn continued to walk and keep Newton from doing his business in the neighbors' yards. Finally, about half a mile from the house she spoke. "We're not partners. I'm aiding an investigation. If you want to turn me in, go ahead."

Eric shook his head. "I don't want to turn you in. I want…" Wanted things to be the way they used to be, but that was impossible. What was done was done. "I think it's clear it's the same attacker from the park. If it's the same guy who killed our victims, though, is blurry. I have enemies, Bryn. So I'm sure you do, too. And while I don't want to bring it up, I think I have to."

Bryn's cheek pulsed as she led them toward a neighborhood park in the heart of the older subdivision. "Bring what up?"

"Have you considered Rand knows you're back in Memphis and could have set this up from inside prison?"

Bryn slowly turned her head toward Eric, utter shock on her face. "No. I don't think my brother set this up. He has no idea that I'm in Memphis. I haven't seen him since the trial."

Eric winced. "I just want to cover all our bases. Any enemies who might know you're here?"

Shaking her head, Bryn closed her eyes. "No. I'm with you, though, on the attacker being separate from the serial killer. It makes the most sense."

"He's treating you differently than the other victims. He didn't strangle them. No marks at all. He never threatened them that we know of. If so, they didn't confide in friends or family." But then Bryn might not have confided any of this if she hadn't been obligated because of her job. Maybe the killer had threatened them physically. No, the women were too smart to keep that hidden.

But Bryn was smart, too, and she hadn't called the police. Eric was completely puzzled.

Newton pranced around the empty park. Not a care in

his puppy world. *Must be nice.* Bryn picked up her pace and let his leash out farther. As her dog released his pent-up energy, she and Eric didn't talk much.

"Okay, Newt, it's time to go home."

Bryn tightened the measure of leash, and they started toward the edge of the road. Headlights came into view.

"Not much traffic in this subdivision. First car I've seen since our walk."

"Playground rarely has kids. I think they've all grown up and moved away." Bryn and Newton made their way into the street to cross. "It's an older neighborhood. I like the fact it's quiet and not littered with children." Her voice quivered on that last statement. At one time, Bryn had loved being surrounded by kids. This was new.

Headlights blinded him. Eric raised his arm over his brow. "What in the world?"

A truck's engine roared.

Reality dawned.

The truck barreled straight for Bryn.

She turned toward it, frozen in the middle of the street. *God, help us!*

"Bryn!" Eric's body kicked into gear, and he sprinted toward her, the truck about five feet away. Diving, he threw his arms around her waist and hurled them onto the edge of the road, feeling the heat from burning headlights against his back. His heart in his throat, they rolled twice, three times into a ditch. Bryn landed on her back, Eric smack-dab on top, shielding her.

He raised his head as brake lights disappeared around the corner. No plate number. No description. Just the fact it was a big red truck.

Bryn's breath came in warm spurts against his cheek, his nose but an inch from hers. Newton yipped, then licked her face. She hadn't let go of that leash.

Eric smoothed the hair that clung to her chin but never

made a move to lift himself from her. The feel of her breathing underneath him, the warmth of her body reminded him she was still alive. It comforted him and slowed his terrified heart rate. "You okay?" he rasped.

She stared into his eyes and nodded. "You?"

"If you are." He pressed his forehead against hers and whispered a prayer of thanks. "Bryn, this guy isn't playing games." He lifted his weight from her, using his arms for fear he'd crush her, but he wasn't ready to lose the connection—the closeness. "He knows where you live."

"I know," she murmured. The flash of panic morphed into soft gratitude. "Thank you. It happened so fast… If you hadn't been…"

He brushed a thumb across her cheek. "But I was." And he would continue to be. No matter what. As much as it pained him to break the connection emotionally and physically, they had to get out of here. The attacker could come back for round two. He stood and took her hands, helping her to her feet. "You sure you're okay? I nailed you pretty good, I think."

"Yeah." She rubbed her lower back, and he noticed a few scuffs on his leather jacket. "You might have been equally as good at football. Ever thought of that?"

Smirking, he pulled his gun out just in case and took her hand with his other, warming to the fact she didn't yank it away. "I have. And I don't mind tackling so much." Especially when it landed him next to her in a ditch. "But I'm not fond of being tackled."

She laughed. "Me, either. But in this case, I'm thankful."

"God saved us."

"Mmm…"

Not excited about kids. Faith shaky at best. What happened? Had Abby's murder killed Bryn's faith, as well? Or had other things piled up? He wanted to ask, but if she wouldn't even tell him why she'd been downtown, she wouldn't open up about more personal feelings. Instead, he walked her home. Outside of Bryn's house, a sleek black Lexus sat in her drive.

"Who in the world is that?"

"I don't know."

Eric inspected the car. No one was inside. He inched toward the front of the house; the glass door was cracked. "Someone's in your house."

Bryn's lips pursed. "I don't have my gun."

"Then stay behind me." Eric slowly inched the wooden door open and quietly turned the knob.

Unlocked.

"Wait," Bryn whispered, but Eric had already stepped inside with his gun ready.

Holt McKnight stood in the living room with a piece of boneless BBQ rib in one hand and an eyebrow cocked. Eric frowned and holstered his weapon. "What are you doing?"

"I own this house. What are *you* doing? Put that gun down and pick up some common sense. You really think a criminal would park their ride in the driveway and enter through the front door...with keys?"

"No. But I wasn't thinking straight since someone tried to make us roadkill just now." Eric told him what happened, ignoring Bryn's perpetual scowl. "And that's my dinner you're eating."

Holt remained calm, skimmed Bryn from head to toe. "You hurt?" He licked BBQ sauce off his thumb as if he hadn't been told his cousin almost died three times, but Eric didn't miss the quiet storm brewing behind Holt's eyes. That was Holt, though. A silent fury.

"No," she barked. "And I don't appreciate you talking about me as if I'm not in the room." She bounced a glare off Eric and stormed to the kitchen.

"Fine. Just so you know, Bryn, I'm about to tell Holt that he needs to stay here with you if you won't let me."

He turned to Holt. "If you aren't going undercover, can you sleep over? I assume that Lexus is an undercover vehicle."

"It is."

Eric dared another glance at Bryn and ignored her seething expression. He'd risk his life for her, and if that meant going against her wishes, then tough.

Bryn didn't mind Holt wolfing down her barbecued chicken or her baked beans. What she did mind was the way fear had frozen her feet to the pavement. She was FBI. Trained. Eric had prayed, but she'd also frozen at offering one up herself even though crying out to God had crossed her mind. She'd had enough rejection so she'd stayed paralyzed—her feet and heart.

This was the third time the assailant had come after her. Twice, Eric had rescued her—even if the first time was indirectly. Dr. Warner was going to assume she wasn't capable enough to stay out in the field. At this point Bryn didn't believe the attacker would leave her alone if she dropped the case. Why did he want her off it? That was strange. *Miss High and Mighty.*

Bryn was rattled. She had to keep a brave front, though. Already the men were going into protective mode, and while the woman in her warmed, the law enforcer had to stick to her guns to prove she was every bit as capable as they were. Her job was riding on this whether they realized it or not.

"I don't need you sleeping over, Holt." She shot a heated glance at Eric. "What happened to 'Bryn is a big girl'?"

Eric wadded his napkin. "Bryn has been almost killed three times. Bryn needs backup."

Holt slid his hands through his midnight-black hair and frowned. "Eric and Bryn need to stop referring to Bryn in third person."

She went for the coffee canister by the pot, but it wasn't

there. *Huh.* She opened the pantry and dug around. What had she done with the coffee? Probably ought to settle for tea the way her nerves were frayed.

Eric cleared the trash from the table. "I'd sleep better if someone was here. Inside."

She snorted. "Yeah, because this is about you and your solid eight hours of shut-eye." Bryn rifled farther back in the pantry. Had she thrown away the canister? Too much crowding her mind. She slammed the cabinet and folded her arms over her chest.

"What are you looking for?" Eric asked and stepped out of her way. She opened the cabinet by the fridge.

"The coffee."

"Where do you keep it?"

"By the coffeepot." She hurried through several more cabinets, then opened the trash can. Maybe she had emptied and tossed it this morning.

Eric covered her hand. The earnestness of his touch silenced her hunt and sent a flush into her cheeks.

"Take a breath." He placed his index finger on her temple, and a lazy grin slid across his face. "You've got too much rolling around in that head of yours."

She inhaled. Exhaled. "I thought I put it on the counter before feeding Newton."

"Where do you keep the dog food?"

"In the laundry room."

Eric stalked from the kitchen into the laundry room near the back door. A minute later, he came out carrying the canister of coffee. "Now, let's make sure you didn't scoop the dog food from this canister and feed Newton coffee grounds, though I'd believe it. He runs on the hyper side."

"So am I or am I not staying?" Holt perched on the counter while Bryn filled the carafe with water. "And do you have any leads?"

Eric groaned. "Waiting on tattoo recognition. That's all

we have right now until we get the note and bullets to the lab, which we're doing ASAP."

"That's pitiful." Holt grabbed an apple from the bowl and twisted the stem in circles. "Might have a better chance canvassing the tattoo parlors. Hit the major ones first. If he's serious about tattoos, he won't let some random dude ink him."

Holt would know. He had several tattoos of his own. None visible with a long-sleeved shirt. "Are you able to stay until we catch this guy?"

"I'll see what I can do. I'm working a Mexican cartel case. I may have to be gone for days." He glanced at Bryn. "So if we're gonna get this house ready for sale, we need to get moving."

Bryn snagged a few mugs from the cabinet and poured a cup. "Saturday. Sunday afternoon, doesn't matter. Unless something comes up."

"I can lend another hand if you want." Eric stirred sugar into his coffee.

Was he offering his help because he and Holt were long-time friends, or was it to keep an eye on her?

"I have a date tomorrow night, but I'm game during the day and on Sunday afternoon." Holt passed on coffee, tossed the apple stem in the trash and scratched Newton's fluffy head.

"Anybody I know?" Eric asked.

"Nah." He wiggled dark eyebrows. "But she looks a little like Piper Kennedy."

"Ransom."

"What?" A dip formed on Holt's forehead.

"She's married. To my partner. Luke *Ransom*."

Holt chuckled. "Oh yeah. I tend to forget that."

Bryn sat her cup down. "You had a thing for Eric's partner's wife?"

Holt shook his head. "She wasn't married at the time.

And not really. She's impressive, though. You should get her to sleep over here. She'd whip a grown man's tail with all her karate moves. She could whip mine."

"She's married," Eric insisted.

"I'm kidding." He rolled his eyes.

Bryn held back the steam wanting to burst through her ears. "I don't need a man or another woman taking care of me. I went through the same training as y'all. You know—forget it." She stormed from the room but caught Eric's voice.

"Dude, you don't know women at all, do you?"

"What? What'd I say?"

Bryn paced her bedroom floor. The carpet was sparse with little padding underneath, but they were ripping it up soon. She slid down on the floor, leaning against the bed. Drawing her knees up, she wrapped her arms around them and stared into nothing. Someone wanted her dead. Again. This was supposed to be a fresh start. She'd be naive to believe that no one would ever target her in this line of work. But this soon, right on the heels of Ohio? Why had God seemed to have stepped out of her life? As if He'd simply checked out on her. So she'd checked out, too, but as she sat in the floor she missed the peace He once brought her.

A knock sounded on the door.

"Go away, Holt."

"Not Holt."

Even worse. Eric ruffled her feathers and ticked her off, but he had a soothing effect on her, too. She didn't have the will to tell him to go away. "Come in."

The door squeaked open, and he tiptoed inside. Bryn continued to stare into space. He slid down beside her, copying her position by locking his arms around his knees. One popped when he drew it up. A telltale sign they weren't getting any younger. Neither had spouses or families. She knew why she didn't. But why hadn't Eric moved on? Or maybe he had.

"Don't you have a girlfriend to get to?" Had she really blurted that out? Yes. Because she needed to know.

"If by girlfriend you mean my TV, then yes. I'm recording a football game, and, no, I do not mean soccer. So don't get smart." He playfully nudged her shoulder with his. "What about you? Anyone special?"

"No."

He leaned his head against the edge of her bed. "Not even a boyfriend here in town?"

"No."

"Sure about that?"

Bryn angled her head to look up at him, but his eyes remained closed, dark lashes spilling across his skin. "I've always been honest with you."

"And I've never lied to you." Something she had always admired about Eric. Honesty, even if it hurt. Oh, and it had. Hurt down deep in her marrow when he told her they couldn't make it work anymore. Couldn't get past what Rand had done to Abby. Not that she hadn't known it as well, but there'd been a sliver of false hope.

"You leave anyone back in Ohio?"

"No. I mean, I dated some but nothing serious. You?"

"Nothing serious."

Jealousy worked its way through her, tugging and squeezing. That wasn't fair. She'd dated, too. But it didn't matter. Someone else had made Eric laugh. Someone else had felt his hand on her lower back as he guided her somewhere wonderful to eat or to a movie. Someone had touched his lips with hers. Which reminded her how soft yet passionate his kisses could be.

Bryn shot up from the floor. "I'm tired."

"I see that." He raised an eyebrow but didn't bother to budge. "What's really eating you?"

Besides his nonserious dating? Or that someone wanted her dead, and she was terrified and even more afraid to admit it? The fact he could read her like an open book? "Why did you tell Holt? He's got enough to worry about with his own job. It's dangerous."

"I'm worried about you. As a colleague and…as a friend."

Friend. It was a step above what they were when she left Memphis. "I hope we can be friends. We haven't cleared the air."

"I don't blame you anymore, Bryn. It was crazy to, but I needed someone to blame because I was hurting."

"So was I," she whispered. "But thank you for that."

He opened his mouth and closed it as if debating something; then he inhaled. "I leaned on God to get me through the pain and to give me strength to forgive. Have you?"

"I tried." Until one bad thing after another kept happening and all her dreams fell into a bottomless pit.

Eric's tender smile nearly had her in tears. A gentle but forlorn look filled his eyes, and he rose and gathered her in his arms, resting his chin on the top of her head.

She hadn't felt this safe and secure in a long time, and yet it ached. Everywhere. "Why this hug?"

"We need it."

Closure? Was he trying to hug some faith into her? Both?

She savored the embrace regardless of the reasons, then slid from it and wrapped her arms around her middle. "I'm not really tired."

"I know," he murmured.

"You wanna go through the photos and reports on the previous victims again?"

"Yeah. And take the evidence to the lab." He opened the door and let her exit first. Holt was stretched out on the couch, eyes closed and breathing deeply.

"Holt," Bryn said. "Holt. *Holt!*" She turned to Eric. "Lotta good he'll do me if someone breaks in."

"I'm awake. Just ignoring you." Holt smirked but kept his eyes closed.

Eric snorted. "We're leaving. Going back to the FO to go over files."

"Ripe hours at the tattoo parlors. Check 'em out."

Holt didn't seem nearly as worried as Eric did, but then he'd become a master at concealing his heart after it had been shattered in high school. Since then, Holt was an impenetrable rock, and something of a skirt chaser, but his wild ways didn't fool Bryn. He was protecting himself. Who knew when or if a woman would crack through his defenses?

"We'll do that."

"I'm already here and too tired to move. See you when you get home."

Baloney. He cared. But he wouldn't tip his hand. "Don't shoot me when I unlock the door."

"Ain't making any promises."

Eric grabbed his keys. "I'll drive."

As they backed out of the driveway onto the street, Bryn eyed a dark sedan parked on the street two houses down.

Eric glanced at her. "What's the matter?"

Bryn swallowed. "Nothing. Just got a lot on my mind."

Like why a car was parked outside a vacant rental home at this time of night and how she could have missed being followed at least twice. Unless the attacker had found out where she lived some other way. But how?

FIVE

Monday morning Eric entered the field office and headed for the major case room with two cups of coffee and a headache. Friday night hadn't panned out as they'd wanted, since they struck out at all four tattoo parlors they'd snooped around in. But that didn't mean they couldn't keep canvassing while they waited for a hit on the database and ballistics and prints to come back. He'd prayed but worry stole his sleep anyway.

Bryn had been less than thrilled when he'd called at 6:00 a.m. on Sunday morning to check in on her.

"Yes, I'm still alive. Holt got a call from the DEA. Didn't say a word about where he was going or when he'd be back, but he said not to worry. Then I saw an SUV outside the house with government tags, so someone was keeping watch. No telling with him.

"How about I bring doughnuts and coffee and help you strip the border in your bedroom? It's gaudy, and, well, it's gaudy."

He'd attended the early service at church, and then shown up with the promised breakfast. By one o'clock, they'd stripped most of it, leaving nothing but yellowed glue stains, which was a step-up from the swan border.

Late afternoon, Eric had played a game of golf with Dad and two of his colleagues at Edgewood. Every second on the green reminded him of Bryn. When it came to her, he'd been set on a hole in one, but he'd sliced and they were doomed to the sand trap—even if stripping border, gorging on doughnuts, listening to terrible disco music and never falling short of conversation had made it seem as if maybe they were digging their way out.

Eric entered the room. Bryn looked up and beamed. "Guess who called?"

Eric slid her requested mocha to her and arched an eyebrow. Guess she needed the extra fluff this morning. "I give up. Who?"

Bryn inhaled the coffee aroma steaming from her cup. "Thanks." She took a sip. "Mr. Danforth. Bridgette's husband. He's in town now. And we have a meeting with him."

"When?"

"Twenty minutes."

"Back to the golf course home? Or his office?"

"Home." She grabbed her jacket and raised her coffee. "Where did you get this?"

"A little place called Bean Me Up. A Trekkie and his sister went into business." He held the door for her. "So good I think it could be futuristic coffee."

Bryn rolled her eyes. "What's this called? The Chocolate Chewbacca?"

Eric froze.

Bryn turned. "What?"

"Chewie is *Star Wars*. You just gave this Jedi a heart palpitation."

"Sure it's not the coffee? It's strong." Bryn winked and stepped into the elevator. "And if I've said it once I've said it a thousand times. You, Eric Hale, are not a Jedi."

"That might be the meanest, low-down, callous thing you've ever said to me." He stepped inside the elevator and held back a grin.

"Well, the coffee's still good." Her lips twitched, and

she brought the cup to her mouth. A mouth he'd loved kissing. But they could never escape the past that had divided them, and his family would never forgive her. Kissing Bryn Eastman was out.

At Mr. Danforth's, Eric rang the bell. They were greeted by Rosalina, the housekeeper who Eric had charmed last time.

"You make me any empanadas?" Eric asked.

"No, senor, but I not forget you."

"I'm kinda unforgettable." Eric motioned for Bryn to follow Rosalina while he brought up the rear. Mr. Danforth sat on a high-back couch, one leg crossed over the other—the shiniest shoes ever on his feet. Did he actually use them to walk? Eric glanced around the house. Everything seemed polished and new. Definitely not a lived-in house. Mr. Danforth stood, dismissed Rosalina and shook Bryn's hand, then Eric's. "I'm shaken up about this." Gray eyes fixed on Bryn. "You have any leads?"

Bryn smiled, but her eyes held suspicion. He'd never seen her interrogate anyone before. Other than him a few times when he was supposed to call her and got hung up at work. *This ought to be interesting.*

"May we have a seat?" she asked.

"Of course. I'm sorry. I flew in first I heard. Been at a business conference for a week."

Bryn held his gaze and waited several beats before she spoke. "What was being married to Bridgette like?"

Mr. Danforth shifted.

"You can be honest. We've ruled you out." Bryn cocked her head.

Ruled him out? They'd just discussed the fact that he had time to leave the conference and return unnoticed if he'd taken a private plane. Eric kicked back and watched Bryn take charge.

"Bridgette was magnetic. I fell fast and hard. But she

was also ambitious and headstrong, as I am. We worked more than we spent time together."

"And you had an affair?" Bryn held her hands up. "I'm not judging. I'm trying to understand who Bridgette was, her motivations."

Mr. Danforth leaned forward, elbows on his knees. "I was lonely. And quite frankly, feeling old. I met Lonnie at the club. One thing led to another."

How many times had Eric heard that? Never boded well. Many times it ended in one or more parties murdered and family members left behind cleaning up the mess.

"Was the divorce civil?"

Mr. Danforth let out a humorless hoot. "Nothing was civil if you crossed Bridgette. She hired that awful Hemingway woman who nearly left me a pauper."

Eric and Bryn exchanged glances. Annalise Hemingway was victim number three. *Interesting information.*

"You seem to have risen above poverty level." Bryn took her time surveying the room, making a point. "What about after the divorce? Any interactions between you two—civil or not?"

"I saw her occasionally. It was cool at best."

"Do you know of anyone who might want to kill her? Did she ever confide in you?"

"Confide? No. Not even when we were married. I wish she had, though." He shrugged. "Anything else I can help with?"

"No. If we have any more questions, we'll contact you."

Rosalina saw them to the door.

Inside the car, Eric shifted toward Bryn, keys in hand. "I wonder if our first two victims also sought Annalise as a divorce lawyer. Marriages have trouble. Not all end in divorce, but—"

"You think someone is killing women who retained or inquired about divorce with Annalise Hemingway?" She chewed her thumbnail. "Why not make her the final target then?"

"I'm saying there's a connection."

"I'd like to see if the mayor's wife ever visited Annalise."

"I don't think the mayor is a serial killer. Not all sociopaths are murderers." Eric whipped out of the drive. "What if our killer doesn't actually do the killing? He could be a watcher. The guy who attacked you might be the muscle behind the string puller."

"Let's hit a few more tattoo parlors. Seedier ones. The popular parlors gave us squat."

He'd hunt down every tattoo parlor in the city if it meant keeping Bryn with him. The longer she was next to him, the safer she'd be. But eventually, they'd have to sleep, and he'd have to let her go back to her house. With only a patrol car outside or Holt sleeping over.

It wasn't a matter of *if* the killer would come back.

But when.

After visiting several ink parlors, talking with the spouses left behind from the first two victims and lunch, the most they'd dug up was some dust from the road.

But Bryn had gained some insight into Kendra Kennick and Cat Weaver. Both women had major cases of OCD. They stuck to their routines—neither of which connected with the other. Whoever abducted them wouldn't have had an issue with where to find them. According to neighbors, they each walked their dogs at the same time each morning and night. Exercise was a five-day-a-week love affair for them both, but they didn't have memberships to the same gym. The only link all the victims might share was the mayor, which was a stretch.

"I feel like we're chasing wind, Eric. After we finish here, let's go to Rhodes College and talk with some of Cat's colleagues. Maybe they'll remember something new. And I'd like to see her records, talk to some of her students."

"Okay." Eric stepped out of the car and adjusted his fitted leather jacket, scuffs on the back and all. Quite the "bad boy" look, but if anyone spent five seconds with him, they'd see he was anything but bad.

Three vehicles filled the tiny lot. Didn't look like three o'clock in the afternoon was prime time for tats. Bryn followed Eric down the sidewalk. "I hope the building isn't any indication of the work they do."

Shoddy. Run-down. A small brick building with a large window displaying the name in neon. Get Inked Body and Piercing Emporium.

"How many customers do you think even know what *emporium* means?" Eric took the concrete stairs leading to the tinted glass door.

"Are you profiling?"

Eric grinned. "No way. I know a really classy lady with a dolphin tattoo on her left shoulder." He winked, and Bryn's cheeks heated.

Bryn followed him inside the ink shop. Black ceiling, red walls. A glossy black counter with a glass case displaying piercing accessories. The buzz of needles raking across skin floated from one of the rooms down the hall.

A husky man with a tattooed bald head stepped around the corner. Every free inch of skin had either been pierced or inked. "Be right with y'all. Have a seat."

Bryn glanced at the black leather chairs with chrome legs and arms lining the walls. Tattoo magazines covered end tables. The room was organized. Art covered the walls, probably original.

Eric approached the counter instead of taking a seat. "Are you the owner or manager?"

"Co-owner. You lookin' for a tat?" He gestured toward Bryn. "Or your old lady?"

With eyebrows raised, Eric gave Bryn an amused smirk. "My old lady here already has one. And I'm not in the market today. However, you can help me." He showed his badge to the co-owner, and the put-out expression that crossed Bald Guy's face couldn't be more obvious.

"We have our licenses. We haven't inked a minor since the last incident. I promise."

Bryn stepped up to the counter. "We aren't interested in minors. I'm looking for a guy who might have been tattooed by you or a colleague. This is on his right hand." She placed the tribal drawing on the counter. "You recognize it?"

Bald Guy picked up the picture. "Yeah. Yeah. That's Jake's design. He's with a client. Hold on, and I'll go get him."

Bryn's insides danced a jig. Finally, they might be getting somewhere after endless dead ends.

The *zzzzzzz*'ing of the needles stopped. Bald Guy came out of the room with Jake. Medium height and build. Tattooed sleeves covering both arms. Hair in a ponytail that hung longer than Bryn's.

"Can you remember who you inked that on?" Bryn pushed the drawing toward him.

He studied it. "Dude wanted a tribal that looked sweet when he fisted his hand. So I delivered."

"Name?"

"Jake." He held out his hand. "I'm Jake Brenning."

Bryn shook his hand and smirked. "Nice to meet you. But I meant what's the *dude's* name."

Jake grinned, straight white teeth flashed. Nice-looking guy. "I can check the file. Give me a minute."

A smug grin continued to cling to Eric's mug.

"What?"

"He knew who you were talking about. He's into you."

Bryn rolled her eyes. "Whatever."

"Okay. But he is. If he doesn't hit on you, I'll buy you dinner wherever you want to go. And if he does, you buy mine."

"Anywhere I wanna go?" Bryn razzed.

"Ha. Ha. I get to choose."

Bryn pointed at him. "Deal."

Jake returned with a file. "Yeah. So I don't have a name. Just remember the dude paying cash, and I kept a copy of my artwork." He held it out. If Bryn had been a better artist, it'd be a perfect match.

"Well, do you remember doing the tattoo?" Bryn asked.

Jake leaned his elbows on the counter. "Vaguely. I do lots of tats. And it's been a couple months. But he was a white guy. Bushy beard but not long. Blondish-brown hair. I think he worked landscaping. Said something about putting in some shrubs at a real…well, not so nice lady's house."

Bryn had a pretty good idea what her attacker had actually said. Probably the same word he'd called her. "He say what landscaping company?"

"No, but he worked for rich chicks. Didn't seem to like them much. I mentioned he ought to find a sugar mama with one of 'em, and he went on a rant about women thinking they can have anything and do anything but then expecting a man to pay for it all. I don't know. I hear stuff, you know?"

"Oh I'm sure." Bryn grinned. "Me, too."

"So we have something in common. You inked?"

"Maybe."

"You are." He winked. "Classy types always have one hidden. Shoulder. Hip." His eyes roamed her form.

Eric cleared his throat. "Anything else? That pertains to the client?"

Jake shook his head. "Nope. Not that I can remember."

Bryn handed Jake her card. "If you remember anything else."

"And what if I want to ask you out for drinks or dinner?"

Eric grinned. "Dinner sounds great. I know exactly where *I'd* pick if she was going with me."

Yeah. Yeah. Bryn had lost. "Business only. But thanks." She stalked out of the parlor to the Durango, ready for the gloating to continue. Took about two seconds.

"So I'm thinking either Folks Folly's or Texas De Brazil. Maybe Flight."

Bryn huffed. "Fine. I owe you dinner. Someday. You didn't say when." She buckled up. "If this guy worked for rich women, I wonder if that's the connection."

"Let's make some calls, see if our victims used the same lawn company."

"You know, I thought they wouldn't go willingly with a guy like that, but if they knew him from their yards, that's a different story." Bryn's heart sped up. They were onto something. Her gut screamed it. By Friday, she'd love to be able to show Dr. Warner solid proof that she was ready and able. What better way than to catch a killer? A killer who wasn't going to rest until Bryn was dead. She had to take him down first. Something pinched her throat and needled her ribs. She couldn't let Ohio repeat itself.

"Hey, what are you thinking?" Eric switched the radio station and pulled onto Madison Avenue.

Bryn forced a smile. "How I'm going to afford feeding you dinner."

Eric chuckled, but his eyes told another tale. He knew she was lying, but he could never know about seeing Dr. Warner or what happened in Ohio. And definitely not what resulted afterward.

Eric itched to pry, but it'd only drive Bryn further inside herself. What was she hiding? It might not be a boyfriend, but she was downtown for a reason—one she wanted to keep private. *God, please help me get her to open up. I'm worried about her. She's changed.*

Bryn held her cell to her ear, scribbling notes and grunting every few seconds. "Great. That's a start. Thanks, Percy." She laughed—a genuine, warm laugh. Wow, he'd missed that sound.

She hung up. "My analyst says that three out of four of our victims used the Grass Is Greener lawn service."

Eric harrumphed. "Guess they found out it wasn't."

Bryn pinned him with a glare.

"It's humor. It's what I do."

"It's subjective." Bryn shoved her phone back in her purse.

She was right. That was ill-humored. But sometimes it just came out willy-nilly. Like the thought "willy-nilly." And it was his coping mechanism. Too much evil out there. "Which one didn't use Grass Is Greener?"

"Cat Weaver."

"Who does Rhodes use to care for the campus lawn?"

Bryn snapped to attention, and her eyes brightened. "I was just sitting here thinking how we were gonna tie them all together. You. Are. Brilliant."

"Aw, now tell me something I don't know."

"You're *not* a Jedi." She yanked her phone from her purse again and hit a button, going to work.

"I *am* a Jedi," he insisted. "And I need an address for this lawn company."

Her mouth twitched, and she handed him her scribbled sheet as she talked a mile a minute to her analyst. "Perfect. Yes." She hung up, a triumphant grin from ear to ear. "Guess who does the lawn service for Rhodes?"

"I give up. Who?" He chuckled. "Let's go find us a dirtbag."

"No better place than a company that sells them."

Eric turned up the radio. "This calls for a celebratory dinner. How about tonight?"

"I know what you're doing." Bryn adjusted the belt on her jacket. "It won't work."

She owed him dinner. He'd get it one way or another. Besides, he wanted to spend more time with her, even though he shouldn't. It was destined to end in heartbreak, probably mutual heartbreak. And he'd made a promise to Dad not to do anything that might bring added stress on Mom. Life was entirely too complicated.

His phone rang. Glancing at the caller ID, he frowned.

"What's the matter?" Bryn tilted her head and studied him.

"Nothing. It's a CI."

"You have a criminal informant on this case?"

He answered on his Bluetooth. "Hey, Angela. Hold on." He muted the earpiece. "Another case." Angela had been handed to him through Holt when he worked a drug case that overlapped a homicide she'd witnessed.

"Okay, what's up?"

"I need to talk to you." A sniff filtered through the line. "Can you come get me?"

"Are you in danger?" He slowed at the stoplight.

"No. I just need to talk to you. Please. It's important. I'm at the Sonic on Frayser-Raleigh Road."

That couldn't be good.

"Sure. Give me about twenty minutes. Traffic's about to get bad."

"Thanks, Eric. You're the only one I can turn to." That was probably the truth.

"Hang tight." He hung up. "Care for a cherry limeade?"

Bryn squinted. "What's going on?"

Eric sighed. "About a year ago one of Holt's cases and mine collided. Angela was a witness. Junkie prostitute. She testified against some gang members. After, she went into rehab and a few women from my church, at my request, helped her get set up in an affordable neighborhood."

"And?"

Eric rubbed the back of his neck. "And she did fine for a while. I've used her in three cases, but then she relapsed. She's in Frayser right now. So I'm thinking she got back with an old pimp. Nothing good is going to come from this."

"How many times did you try to get her clean?"

"Every time she's asked. And I'll keep doing it. I have to. One of these days, it'll take. Praying it will anyway."

"You're a good man. You know that, Eric Hale?"

"I do. Pat myself on the back every day," he teased. Angela reminded him so much of Abby. Instead of helping Abby break free of drugs, he'd arrested her, thinking tough love would work. No mercy. All it did was build a wall. And then she died before he could ever apologize and make things right.

But he could help Ang.

Fifteen minutes later, Eric wheeled into a space at Sonic. Angela sat at one of the red metal tables under the canopy. Her bleached-blond hair had grown out, leaving several inches of dark roots. She'd lost weight. Couldn't be more than a hundred pounds and that was counting the frayed jeans and bomber jacket. It wasn't quite cold enough for it, but Eric doubted she had anything else.

"Should I stay in the car?" Bryn asked.

"No, come on. She'll trust you if you're with me. And who knows? I might need a woman for this."

The smell of burgers and fries hung in the air as Sonic servers zipped along on Rollerblades. Angela's eyes widened as she spotted Bryn. She wrung her hands in her lap, chipped black polish on every finger.

"This is a friend of mine, Angela. Bryn Eastman."

Bryn smiled. "Nice to meet you." Compassion slid through her soft voice. "Can I have a seat?"

Angela sniffed and wiped her nose with the back of her

hand. Her nose wasn't running, though. Looked like cocaine use again. "Sure. Yeah."

"When's the last time you ate, Ang?" Eric asked and sat next to her, sandwiching himself between the women. One smelled of stale smoke and hops and barley while the other smelled like a grove of sunshiny oranges and vanilla dreams.

"I…um… I don't know."

Eric pressed the speaker button. "Burger, chicken or dogs?"

Angela held her stomach. "It all sounds nauseating."

"You need to eat."

"Chicken."

Eric ordered a chicken sandwich combo with fries and two coffees for himself and Bryn. "What's up? Why you out here in Frayser? You with Trey again?"

"No. I mean, I see him some, but I'm not working for him. I set my own rules. Came out here to see a friend." She gnawed on her lip, and a tear spilled down her cheek. "I'm pregnant, Eric. Again."

Eric kept a cool exterior. Angela had been to a clinic several times to have an abortion. But she'd promised to be consistent with her birth control. He should've known better.

Bryn slipped her hand over Angela's. "Do you know who the father is?"

Angela picked at her nail polish. "A regular. I haven't… I haven't worked a corner in a few months. He takes care of me, you know? He's good to me. I thought maybe he'd want a baby together. He's going to leave his wife. He promised."

And Eric had wings to fly. "Have you told him?"

Angela covered her face and cried. "He said I can't. But I want this one. I do."

Eric ran a hand over the stubble on his chin. "That all he say?"

Angela rubbed her nose and sniffed again. The food came. After handing them the condiments, Eric popped a peppermint in his mouth.

"When I told him I was keeping the baby, he went wild. I know he'll come around but… I need a place to stay. He kicked me out of the apartment he rented for me."

Yellow-and-purple bruises peeked from the edge of her coat collar. If he'd put his hands on her, knowing she was carrying a child, there was no telling what else this jerk might do. "I need a name."

"No. I just need a place to stay until I figure out what to do next."

Too scared to cough up his identity. "Let me call around and see if I can get you into an unwed mothers' home. Or some kind of program. If you want to have this baby, Angela, you can do it. And you should. But no more drugs."

"I promise. I'm gonna clean up. I will."

"Give me a name. I can't protect you if I don't know who you need protecting from."

"No. He's important and he's got kids and stuff. It'll only make him madder. If you make me tell you…I'll, I'll run." She clawed at her hair and rocked back and forth.

"Where you gonna go, Ang? You don't have any family." His heart sank to his feet, and he silently prayed for wisdom and strength.

Bryn laid a gentle hand on her shoulder. "Breathe. Getting worked up isn't good for you. Or the…the baby." Her face twisted with emotion. Sympathy. Compassion. Something else. The way she cared about people warmed him.

"I gotta get outta Memphis." She shoved the bag away. "Just for a while until he comes around."

Mystery Man wasn't going to come around. But if he was as important as she said, he might try to shut her up, permanently. "I'll call Patty and see if she can help us get you in somewhere." And far enough across the state line to keep her safe. "You'll be closer to the church at least."

She dropped her head.

"No judgment from me, Ang. I just know how much you liked it when you went. No one is going to look down on you for being pregnant."

Angela ripped the foil on her chicken sandwich and nibbled. "I know," she whispered.

"Have you seen a doctor?" Bryn asked.

She shook her head and broke off a piece of chicken.

"You need to. You're not taking care of only yourself now." Bryn stood. "Excuse me. I need to make a phone call."

Eric half stood. "I'll be there in a minute."

Bryn hurried to the car. Eric switched gears and focused on Angela. "I have a friend who can help you. She can get you set up with a doctor."

Angela clutched Eric's hand. "I'm scared. I hate being alone."

"I know. But you're not alone. And no one is going to hurt you. I promise."

"I'm still not giving you a name."

"I understand. But let me be clear, you are under no circumstances to have contact with this man by phone, text, email or in person."

Angela nodded. "Okay."

"If he calls or texts, ignore it. I can't fight a ghost, Ang. The only way to protect you is to cut off your contact and move you. I'll get on that today. In the meantime…" He glanced toward the car. No, he couldn't put her up with Bryn. Too much danger already. "I'll put you in a hotel until we can work something out."

"Thanks, Eric. I knew you'd help me."

"Come on." He grabbed the two cups of Red Button coffee and waited as Angela bagged up her food, then he led her to the car. She opened the door and slid in. Bryn stretched across the seats and opened his door, taking her cup.

"Everything okay?" he asked.

"Yeah. Good. Just needed to make a call."

He wasn't buying that for a dollar. "Okay. I need to get Angela settled in a hotel, and then we can head to the Grass Is Greener."

"Sounds like a plan."

Sounded like Bryn was hiding things again.

SIX

Bryn squirmed in the passenger seat of the Durango while Eric checked Angela into a hotel room. Far away from this important man—the man who'd hurt Angela and probably threatened her life for wanting to have a baby. How was this young woman going to raise a baby?

Eric was invested in Angela. He'd always had a generous and compassionate heart, but he'd been tough on Abby when she spiraled into drugs. But then weren't people tougher on the ones they loved most? Expected more from them?

Dad's military background had spilled into their family life. He'd been especially hard on Rand. But Bryn didn't blame Dad's strict rules for Rand's demented behavior. Eric thought he'd been the one behind these attacks from his prison cell. Bryn hadn't wanted to believe it, but she'd called and checked the visitor logs. No one had come to see him. He'd had three cell mates. One was dead and the other two were still on the inside. It wasn't Rand.

What made a man a monster? Was he born that way? Environment? Both? Neither? Bryn had spent hundreds of hours poring over books written by professionals, as she tried to wrap her brain around her brother's mind. A boy who grew up with her and carried a bloodlust.

When she failed to figure him out, she knew the victims

would speak louder and clearer than the masquerading evil ever would. They didn't hide like the monsters that claimed their lives. That's how she tracked killers—through studying the victims.

Angela spoke to her. A victim. Probably came from an abusive and poor economic background. No father figure or a lousy one at best. Whoever the important man was, he preyed on her insecurities and need for a father, a need for unconditional love. He'd used and abused her. And Angela defended him, wrapped in her delusions and his deception.

Bryn closed her eyes. Thousands of women out there wanted babies and couldn't have them, while women like Angela easily conceived. Where was the fairness in that?

She opened her eyes and stared out the window. As the day had worn on, the light gray sky had deepened to charcoal. The temperature had dropped into the high fifties, but the wind with its bitter whipping made it feel more like forties.

Eric stepped outside the hotel, hair blowing in disarray. He'd never worn it close-cropped; it lightly touched the collar of his jacket and covered the tops of his ears. Thick and finger-running worthy.

He jumped in the driver's side. "I hate winter."

"It's not winter."

He frowned and cranked the heat, then retrieved a Twizzler from his inside jacket pocket. "I wonder if I could work for the Florida police department in fall and winter, then transfer back for spring and summer."

Bryn clicked her seat belt in place. "So how's Angela?"

"Shaken up. Still won't tell me who the father is. Truth is, she might be lying just for help. I've moved her to three apartments in the last nine months. But I can't give up on her."

Did he mean Angela or Abby?

"How far along is she?" Traffic crept along as if no one was hurt, dead or fighting for survival. Business as usual.

"She thinks she's almost four months. Doesn't look pregnant at all to me. That can't be good, right?"

How would she know? She'd never been pregnant. "You call a friend to get her into a doctor?"

"Yeah. Patty's going to get her an appointment and take her to see about some government help. I thought she was going the straight and narrow this time." Disappointment filtered through his words. "I'm worried about the baby. She's using. I can tell."

Bryn cringed. "That baby doesn't have a fighting chance."

"I'm praying. Praying God will bring the baby to term, and she'll get it together and be a good mom. Patty said she was going to talk to the home for unwed mothers. They work with a Christian-based rehab. And they help women find jobs." He shrugged. "Maybe Ang can get in there."

Ang.

Was he using Angela as a surrogate sister? "You did what you thought was right with Abby," she whispered. "You know that, don't you?"

Eric's grip on the wheel tightened. "I'm not mad at you or anything, but I don't want to talk about Abby or the drug use…or how I handled it."

Bryn rubbed her arm as if wiping off the sting his statement made. "I'm sorry."

"Don't be. Let's see if we can take our minds off things by catching us a killer today and keeping you safe."

Nothing sounded better. "I hope we don't spook him when we waltz in there. You have the cop swagger."

Eric frowned. "I do not."

"Do." They needed a cover. "I think we should go in as a couple looking for mums or something."

"Mums or something?" He eyed her, then grinned. "Okay. Not like we don't have experience."

Bryn's heart constricted. *A couple.* Time to thin out the air that had thickened in the vehicle. "We never planted mums."

At the stoplight, he shifted toward her; his voice softened. "You know what I mean."

Bryn's throat constricted. "Yeah."

Twenty minutes later, Eric backed into a space near the exit. "Do I look like a cop?"

"Not until you walk." She chuckled and stepped out of the car. Eric came around and laced his fingers in hers. Still a perfect fit. Her stomach opened the gate for a swarm of butterflies to take flight.

"For disguise." He tossed her a lopsided grin. "You okay with this?"

No. Not. At. All. It reminded her of everything they'd been together and everything they'd lost. He couldn't even talk about Abby with her. Any sliver of hope was gone. "Sure." She leaned in and wrapped her free arm around his biceps, giving the illusion of a happy couple.

Eric stiffened for a second, then relaxed.

"*You* okay?" she asked.

"Yeah. Sure. Let's putter around before going to the counter."

"Good idea."

Outside the giant brick building, a fall rainbow of mums lined shelves and walkways. Trays of blue, yellow and violet pansies brightened the cloudy day. They passed shrubs and lawn equipment. Patio tables surrounded by chairs with brown and rust-colored designs for fall enticed her eyes.

"You still live in Germantown?"

"Yep." He released her hand and sat in a wrought iron chair, rocked back and forth. "I could use some new patio furniture."

The warmth from his hand in hers evaporated, leaving her cold and empty. She sat across from him. "I thought you had wooden furniture?"

"I do. But they don't rock."

Eric had purchased a huge home a year after they began dating exclusively. Bryn had believed it was in preparation for a proposal and for a future with a big family. One that never came. Did he feel lonely living in a thirty-five-hundred-square-foot home with five bedrooms, an in-ground pool and a hot tub? Wonder if he ever used the double oven set in the brick wall. Doubtful.

A worker in dirty jeans, steel-toed boots and a heavy jacket caught Bryn's eye. "He's dressed a lot like the guy who attacked me."

Eric darted his glance toward the smooth-skinned worker, then checked the price tag on the chairs. "What do you think? Wanna look around some more?" His voice raised and carried. The guy looked their way.

"Y'all need some help?"

"Just looking for some new furniture for the…old lady." Eric eyes swam with playfulness, and he leaned over and tugged a strand of her hair. "Aren't we, babe?"

Babe. Could have jumped back in time. He'd called her babe so often. Had it slipped out or was it intentional? "Yeah," she said through a clogged throat. She couldn't even muster a snarky comeback to the *old lady* remark.

The guy moved along. After a few more pass-throughs, they made their way to the counter. Bryn glanced around. "I'm going to look at a few trees for the front yard while you talk to the manager," she said for the cashier's sake.

Eric held on to her coat sleeve. "Not a good idea. Let's do it together."

"Don't trust my judgment?"

Eric's right eyebrow slid north. "I trust you fine. But I'd hate for someone to talk you into something you don't want."

Eric might not want her to search for the tattooed attacker alone, but if anyone suspected or overheard Eric's conversation with the manager, they might tip him off. She needed to find him first. She patted her purse. "I've got my phone. I'll call you if I need help." That is, she had her gun this time and was on the offense.

"Can I help you two?" The cashier gave them a quizzical look.

"My husband wants to talk to the manager about a discount on a table with some scratches. I'm going to check out shrubbery for the front yard." She scurried off before Eric could protest. Up and down the aisles, searching. She pushed through swinging doors to the outdoor area.

In the distance she spotted a bushy-bearded guy with the same build, boots and tattoo.

Bingo!

Eric cringed, but making a scene wasn't an option. Why was Bryn so stinking stubborn? Truth be told, he was as frustrated with himself as he was with Bryn for going rogue in an outdoor center. Why did he have to take her hand? He'd played into the act more than necessary, pretending for a moment it was real. Leaning over to touch her hair, allowing himself to revel in the silkiness, letting her pet name, *babe*, roll off his tongue. It'd felt natural. Right. And it had ignited a fire in his gut that had been smothered for the past several years.

The professional lines had blurred. He had no choice but to reel in his personal feelings. When this case was over, Bryn would go her own way, and they'd more than likely never see each other again. It was time to snuff them out. He shouldn't put it off until they were finished working together.

But could he?

The manager, a woman in her early to midthirties came through doors marked Employees Only with a smile on her face. "How can I help you?"

Eric glanced at her name badge. Allison Landers. The cashier busied himself with a patron. Eric removed his badge and held it up. "I need to talk to you about an employee. I don't have his name, but he has a tribal tattoo on the top of his hand. Beard."

Allison grimaced. "Rusty Beckham. What's he done? Is it drugs?" She sighed. "Follow me. We can talk in my office." She escorted him through the private doors, down a tiled floor into a typical office space.

"You say he has problems with drugs?"

"I've heard rumors, but he's passed all the tests given according to his file. We surprise all our employees with drug tests. We can't have them on the job high as kites and working equipment. Most of our services cater to wealthy home owners."

"You have a photo of Rusty?" Not that he'd be able to clearly identify him. Bryn hadn't actually seen his face. But he needed something to go on.

"Sure." She stood and opened a filing cabinet drawer. "All our employees have photos taken and background checks. Rusty comes to work faithfully, does a good job and doesn't say too much. At least to me. But I'm new. Just took over about three weeks ago, moved here from Little Rock. Last manager transferred to the store in Jackson."

Allison handed Eric the file. "Rusty's been on the job for the last five years."

Eric jotted down a physical address. "He working today?"

"Yes. He did an outside job this morning, but he's here now. Or should be."

And Bryn was out there. The store was huge, and that wasn't counting the outdoor area with trees, mulch, flowers and lawn equipment, as well as machinery and a small tree nursery. He could be anywhere.

She could be anywhere.

His stomach tightened. "I need to see a list of residents he worked for within the last year."

Allison nodded. "Sure. What's he done?" She clacked the keyboard, and the printer came to life.

"Maybe nothing. Just a person of interest."

She grabbed a sheet. "This is every house he's worked in the last year. Addresses and phone numbers."

"Thanks." Eric scrolled the list. A sour taste coated his tongue. Kendra Kennick, Annalise Hemingway and Bridgette Danforth had been residents where Rusty had worked. And Rhodes College was listed as a client, as well. "This is what I needed." A link that connected Rusty Beckham to each victim.

"Should I call him to the front? Is he in trouble?" Worry filled her eyes.

"No. Just go on business as usual. What area does he usually work in when he's in the building?"

Allison shrugged. "Could be anywhere. Loading machinery, helping mulch, making mulch or hosing off dirty aisles. Employees that do outside jobs supplement hours by working where they're needed at the time."

"I'll find him. Appreciate your cooperation."

If Rusty had been rumored to do drugs, would Holt have heard of him?

The better question at the moment was, where was Bryn?

An urge to find her sent adrenaline racing through him, and he stalked up and down aisles, the earthy smell of mulch and dirt enveloping his senses. He hopped over garden hoses and rounded corners, customers and a few workers. No Rusty Beckham. No Bryn.

He pushed through swinging doors that led to the outdoor nursery area. Beyond the shrubs and small trees was the mulching area. High-powered machinery parked next to tree limbs and mountainous piles of mulch. Eric scanned the area. No one. In fact, it was eerily quiet.

He weaved through rows of sapling trees, ground coverings, shrubs and pots of various sizes and shapes. Where was she?

Where was Rusty?

A wave of nausea drove through his stomach and into his chest, tightening it. She had her gun. And, yes, Bryn was a big girl, fully capable, but Rusty had the upper hand here. He knew the store inside out. Eric inhaled and exhaled. Paranoia was getting the best of him. Bryn was fine. She was careful.

But Rusty knew her face. Bryn didn't know his. If he was wearing gloves, she'd have no way to identify him.

An overwhelming need to call out her name swept over him, but he clamped his jaw shut and worked through the tractors, lawn mowers, tillers and various machinery.

A loud rumbling noise came to life. Eric shifted left. A figure bolted from beyond the heavy-duty machinery.

Eric couldn't be sure if it was Rusty Beckham or not. Didn't matter. Running was never good. Eric sprinted after him, hurdling several mowers, then slid to a halt. Why wasn't Bryn in pursuit? If Rusty had made her but she hadn't seen him, why run? Why not sneak away and avoid a scene?

Eric backtracked to the noise that had suddenly kicked on before Rusty made a break for it. An industrial-size tub grinder that turned trees and limbs to mulch was loaded to the brim, but he couldn't see inside. It was too high. What if she was in there? He didn't have time to search elsewhere. Not if Rusty had tossed her inside. *God, help me!*

Eric's heart kicked into overdrive, his legs powered ahead nearly taking his feet out from under him. "Hey! Hey!" he hollered at anyone, no one. How was he going to turn off the oversize wood chipper?

Couldn't think about that now. He needed to get up in there. And fast.

Limbs and branches grated and cracked while the long crane at the front of the machine rumbled and spit flecks of mulch into a pile on the ground. With each second, the wood stacked in the mouth of the grinder continued to dwindle.

Sweat ran in streams down his temples and slicked down his back.

"Bryn!" Eric screamed over the motor's roar and the sound of wood being splintered through metal grinders.

The ladder to the empty driver's box was missing. How was he going to climb up there?

Time might be running out. His breath shallow, he darted his gaze around the eight-foot-high machine; he flew out of his leather coat, and climbed onto the axle leading to the driver's box. He shimmied up it until he made it to the back of the glassed-in driver's area.

Eric needed a better look, but first he needed to turn it off in case she was lodged somewhere inside.

He scrambled on top of the driver's box, then swung his feet into the open area, landing with a crash onto the seat. Gadgets and gears blurred. No key? Really?

He glanced up again. The wood had sunk even farther into the mouth of the beast, the pile on the ground building with every second.

With shaking hands, he ran his fingers across the gadgets until he found a black lever on the floor near the leather seat.

God, don't fail me now!

He slammed it forward, and the machine slowly powered down until it was silent.

Now to see if she was inside. If she wasn't, where was she?

He clambered back on top of the driver's box, then dropped about four feet onto some kind of car that stretched about nine feet before connecting to the actual tub that held the wood. Scrambling to the lip he leaned over.

"Bryn!" He jumped inside, wood needling his sides, ripping his T-shirt, digging into his flesh. Bits of trees slid into his fingers as he clawed through the rubble, tossing away debris from the tub.

But Bryn wasn't inside.

Where was she? "Bryn," he hollered and surveyed the area below him. Rusty wouldn't have run unless Bryn had spotted him. And she hadn't given chase. So she had to be somewhere. But was she safe?

Dread soured his stomach. Frantic he continued to search.

A strand of hair, or what looked like hair, peeked out from a second woodpile about ten feet from this one.

He jumped to the ground and grunted, then raced to the mound.

Bryn lay covered in a pile of branches. Unmoving.

Eric dug through the limbs that had been placed on top of her.

"Bryn!"

She didn't move. *No. No.*

He cleared the debris from her and dropped to his knees. "Bryn," he choked. "Can you hear me?"

God, please don't let her be dead! Let her be okay. Please. Please.

When he'd removed the last log resting across her body, he nearly collapsed. Blood trickled down her face and matted her hair in a sickly sight. He checked her pulse. Faint but there.

"You were supposed to be careful, Bryn," he mumbled more to himself as he gently stroked her cheek.

A moan escaped her lips.

"Er... Eric..."

She was calling. For him. Nothing made him want to save her more. "I'm right here."

"Eric?"

"Don't move. Where does it hurt?"

"My head. My…my back. It stings."

He rolled her to her side and raised the back of her shirt. Scratches. Blood. He breathed a sigh of relief. Didn't look like anything more than superficial wounds.

"Stay put. I'm gonna call an ambulance."

"No, please don't. I'm fine."

"You don't look fine." He hovered over her, brushed matted hair from her face.

"Did you see him?" She sat up, clutching her head. "I might be a little dizzy." She moved her arms and legs. Turned her neck side to side. "But I'm in working order."

Eric rubbed her shoulder. "He has a name. Rusty Beckham. And I saw him, but when I didn't see you giving chase, I circled back around here. Glad I did. Looks like he knocked you out and hid you here, then turned on the grinder to make me think you were inside, giving him time to escape. He'd know I'd climb up and turn it off, then check to be sure. Scared me half to death."

"Me, too." Her hands shook, and she balled them into fists by her sides, continuing to lean into him.

"I won't call an ambulance, but you have to let me take you to the ER to get checked out."

She reached up and touched his cheek; his pulse that had calmed down galloped once more. "Thank you. You saved my life. Again."

Eric would rather catch this guy so no one would have to rescue her and she'd be safe. He clasped her hand resting on his cheek. "Can you stand?"

"I think so." She touched the side of her head and winced. "I didn't think he saw me, but he must have. Guess he hid behind the machine, then doubled back. Whacked me in the head before I even saw it coming." Lips pursed, venom clouded her eyes.

"You've got a hard head. Came in handy today." He lightly clipped her chin and smiled. Losing her like that... He couldn't begin to picture life without her in it. He grabbed his jacket from the ground. "I have an address." He picked up his phone and put out a "Be on the lookout" or BOLO on Rusty Beckham.

"Then let's go find him."

"After we visit the emergency room."

Bryn groaned and leaned against him as he wrapped an arm around her. "Are you going to bring up somebody staying with me again?"

"Nope."

"Really?" She lifted her head to look up at him, a skeptical expression in her eyes.

"No need. You just did." Without thinking it through, he leaned down and kissed her forehead.

SEVEN

Bryn's eyes blinked open, and yesterday's events flooded back. Once again, Rusty Beckham had gotten to her. A millisecond of understanding had hit her before something hard struck her. The memory of the attack in Ohio reared its ugly head. *Shake it off, Bryn. It's over. You're past that.* Bryn wasn't proving she could handle this guy. She hadn't handled Scott Mulhoney, either. Not without losing part of herself.

She had to be more alert. Next time Rusty might actually accomplish his goal.

Eric had sat with her as the doctor examined and diagnosed her with a concussion. Which meant rest for twenty-four hours. If Eric hadn't shown up and rescued her... She shuddered.

"Hey, you're awake." Eric smiled and brought her a mug, steam rising from the center. She shifted on her couch and scooched up. "What time is it?"

"It's nine. How do you feel?"

Had he spent the night? He was with her when she fell asleep, and someone had pulled her from sleep all too often, annoying her. But the doctor had instructed someone to wake her every hour.

"Is she up?" Holt stumbled into the living room, sleepy-eyed and hair a disaster. Girls probably loved that look.

"I'm up." She accepted the warm mug from Eric. Tea. "Did you stay the night?"

"We both did. I took the guest room with a bed. Holt bunked in your bed."

"We alternated rousing you. You're mean when you don't get your sleep, which is why we left you on the couch. Not worth the fight." Holt smirked. "Dude, I'm not drinking tea."

Eric grinned, looking fresher and way more bushy-tailed than Holt. "There's a pot of coffee on."

"Your hair's wet. You used my shower?" Bryn sipped her tea and tried not to feel weird about that. Seemed intimate.

"No. I did your seven o'clock wake up and then went home and showered." Guess he thought it might be too intimate, as well. He cleared his throat. "I've been back about thirty minutes."

"Bryn, do you not grocery shop?" Holt hollered from the kitchen.

"I have eggs."

Holt strode into the living room with a cup of coffee. His jeans were as rumpled as his hair, his scruff thicker. He dropped into the recliner. "I burn eggs. Can we call in a pizza?"

"At nine in the morning? No." Bryn rubbed her head. Fuzzy and throbbing, but the stabbing pains had dissipated. "Thank you for the tea, but we've got a long day, and I'll need something stronger." She stood on wobbly legs and waited for some balance before making her way to the kitchen. "Where's Newton?"

Eric pointed to her puppy fast asleep at the foot of the couch. "He hasn't left your side."

Neither had Eric it appeared. Bryn could get used to that. But she wouldn't.

"You don't plan on working today, do you?" Eric followed her into the kitchen, leaning against the counter as she poured the strong brew.

"I do. We have an address to check out. Any news on the BOLO? They find Rusty Beckham?"

Eric shook his head. "Had unmarked cars outside his apartment—still do. He never showed up. Probably shacking up at a friend's or girlfriend's. We have a warrant to search his place. Did find out what kind of vehicle he drives. A red F-150."

That could have been the truck that tried to mow them down. It had been dark. "I didn't get any hits on him," Holt said as he entered the kitchen. "Checked with a few CIs. They don't know him." He finished his coffee and poured another cup. Black.

Guess Rusty didn't have any drug connections. Eric had filled her in at the ER, although some of what he'd said was hazy. "I'm gonna get dressed, and we can head that way." She put her hand up before Eric had the chance to give her grief. "If I feel like I'm going too hard, I'll stop. I promise." She carried her mug and inched toward her bedroom.

"I don't believe you, you know," Eric called.

Bryn grabbed Holt's shoes and tossed them into the kitchen. "Thanks, guys." They'd kept vigil couch-side all night. It moved her, and tears stung the backs of her eyes. More than she wanted to admit, more than she would admit, she needed them. Both of them.

Once again she'd almost died. A trembling came over her as she sank down the wall in her bathroom and cried. What would Dr. Warner say? Would this second attack chain her to a desk? Maybe she did belong there. She closed her eyes and saw Scott Mulhoney standing over her. Pulling the trigger. Where had God been during that?

She slipped into black flat-heeled boots and grabbed her own black leather jacket. Her other coat needed a trip to the dry cleaner.

She entered the living room. "Let's go. Before you ask, I'm fine."

Without a word, Eric led the way to the Durango.

Rusty Beckham's apartment was a shoddy crackerjack box in a run-down neighborhood. Inside, empty pizza boxes lined the counters, and beer cans littered the table next to a faded green recliner facing a forty-two-inch flat-screen TV. Bryn flipped through the DVDs. Nothing but filth degrading women. "This explains where he learned such gentlemanly behavior," she spouted.

Eric glanced at the movies. "Classy." He snapped his latex gloves several times as he trolled the living room and kitchen. "Even classier magazines." He held one up with the tips of his fingers as if touching it might infect him somehow.

Bryn turned her nose up and riffled through Rusty's mail. *Interesting.* "What's this?"

Eric towered behind her, leaving her hyperaware of his nearness, his clean scent and understated cologne. "M.A.G.E. Never heard of it."

"Looks like a newsletter for an organization." Bryn opened it. The letterhead revealed a gender sign—a circle with an arrow pointing from the top right and a plus sign sticking out from the bottom. Inside, an equal sign with a slash had been drawn through it.

"Someone doesn't like women," Eric said.

She scrolled through the newsletter. M.A.G.E. turned out to mean Males Against Gender Equality, and the president of the misogynistic coalition—Julian Proctor—was speaking at a rally on Friday night.

Bryn wanted to crumple the paper in her fist and chuck it across the room.

"Yep, he hates women."

Bryn grunted. "Strong women… Wait." She faced Eric. "That's it. That's what links them. We knew they were high-profile women, but they're strong, and together they have a wide range of influence in the community. A tenured professor who chairs several boards at the university, the public relations consultant—she had all sorts of power with the knowledge she possessed about her clients. Annalise Hemingway—only representing women would tick this guy off to begin with, but to take those men for everything they're worth? He'd see that as humiliation. And Bridgette Danforth? Talk show host that had access to every home with a TV."

"And you, Bryn. You came in and took the lead on a case that belonged to a man—"

"I didn't take your case."

Eric held his hands up in surrender. "I know. But Beckham wouldn't see that. He was there that night. Watching. You came bursting on the scene in your FBI windbreaker. Rusty must have thought you were taking over the case... from a man. It infuriated him until he couldn't control himself, and he attacked you in a rage."

"But the note was a threat to back off. I'm not sure the gunfire was intended to kill me now that I really think about it. And he might not have actually meant to run me over, only scare me. I can't be sure. And he didn't actually throw me in the wood chipper."

"Maybe he just didn't think he had the time."

Bryn's blood ran cold, draining from her face and leaving her light-headed. She grabbed the end of the couch to steady herself.

"What is it, Bryn?"

She'd have to fight the paralyzing fear. A panic attack framed the edge of her chest sending palpitations into her throat. She refused to be a victim. Again.

The man hated women for being successful. For taking up a career. He'd made it his mission to destroy them and remove them from the earth, from people they cared about it. People they loved.

"Nothing."

"Your head messing with you?"

More than he could even imagine. She inhaled deeply and exhaled a few times, then shoved the fear down deep. "I'm okay." She made her way to the bedroom. "He's messy. Unorganized. His emotions, mostly hate and anger, fuel him. Like you said, in a rage he came after me with swarms of officers on the scene. All of these deaths are meticulous. Organized. Emotion fuels them, but the killer has complete control, which is how he likes it. The profile doesn't fit with Rusty Beckham, Eric."

Eric opened a nightstand drawer. Bagged a gun for evidence. "I still say it could be two of them. What if someone with more control *is* using him to do the dirty work and likes to watch as Rusty drowns them?"

Possibly. She turned toward the living room and held the newsletter in her hand. "Someone like Julian Proctor?" She pulled her phone from her coat pocket and called Percy. "I want everything you have on Julian Proctor, president of the Males Against Gender Equality coalition. Turn over the rocks, all of them. I want to know what crawls out. And I want to know everything about this M.A.G.E. from financial backing to members. Also, see if you can cross-reference him with Rusty Beckham. I'm curious if we can make a connection between the two."

"Consider the rocks rolled, Agent Eastman. I love stomping creepy crawlers." He hung up.

They continued to dig around the apartment. After about twenty minutes, Bryn's phone rang. Percy. She put him on speakerphone.

"Agent Eastman, I cross-referenced the two names. Rusty Beckham got into an altercation with a man about six months ago outside a women's convention. He was arrested for assault and battery. Guess who bailed him out?"

Bryn turned to Eric and grinned. "Julian Proctor."

"I'm emailing you all the information I dug up on Proctor. He's the number one cardiothoracic surgeon in the United States."

Interesting. "They aren't blood kin? Proctor's not a friend of Beckham's daddy or something like that?"

"Nope. That's all I have between the two."

After thanking him, Bryn hung up. "That's a solid connection."

"Why would the best cardiothoracic surgeon in the United States want to bail out a lowlife like Rusty Beckham?"

"Maybe he was acting on orders or he did it on Julian's behalf. A guy who would be that loyal is worth having around. Worth putting them in debt to you. Beckham probably idolizes Julian Proctor—sees him as a hero, a father figure, a god even. Or all the above. Either way, we need to pay Proctor a visit. Just ask a few questions to feel him out."

If he was behind these murders and the attacks on Bryn, they'd have to be two steps ahead of this crafty snake. One misstep and they both might end up dead.

"You mind if we swing by the church? Patty is working on some camp stuff, and I need to pick up the paperwork." Eric nursed his Starbucks and slowed at the light.

Bryn scrolled through her emails on her phone. "Sure." She pointed at the screen. "I'm reading through the information Percy sent on Julian Proctor. He fits the profile." Bryn grimaced. "His profession gives him power to keep a heart pumping. Power of life and death to an extent."

"God complex?"

"Possibly. Probably. Rusty could have given Julian a list of his clients. Then, after Julian chose the target, Rusty would have had the motivation he needed to hunt them. It would have been easy. The women adhered to daily routines. Rusty or Julian, or the both of them together, could have stalked the victims."

Just like Bryn had been tracked downtown to the place she wouldn't cough up. Had Julian been watching from a safe distance along with Rusty that night at the park?

Bryn continued. "Apparently, the coalition formed about nine years ago. Before that, Proctor was involved with a few radical groups, but nothing the public could discover. Percy has crazy, mad skills."

Eric placed his coffee in the cup holder. "This coalition have a website?"

"No. Which means members hear by word of mouth. We know they receive a newsletter to keep them informed and updated. They don't protest. I'm not sure what they do. Except gather together and hate on women."

"Haters gonna hate." Eric chuckled. "How old is this guy?"

"Fifty-six. Good shape. Belongs to a gym. Never been married. Mother deceased. Father in a nursing home in Madison, Mississippi. He's from Jackson. Wealthy background. His dad was a doctor. Internal medicine."

Eric listened as Bryn rattled off Julian Proctor's background, address and boards he sat on. Sounded like an upstanding citizen. Minus his affinity for hating women. "I find it hard to believe that the hospital would accept his practices."

"Freedom of speech, and I'm sure since he's the number one surgeon, they overlook his extreme prejudice. Then again, with no website, they can't technically connect him to anything unless they get the newsletter. Percy says there's no literature with his picture on it. He signs the newsletters, though, and makes public appearances at these meetings.

I would say he's not hiding his agenda, but he's discreet enough that it hasn't brought much attention, if any, to him."

Eric mused over the man and his beliefs. "Do you think women can do anything men can?"

"Why? You don't?"

"Can you pick up a two-hundred-pound man and carry him half a mile if you have to?"

"Are you for this guy?" Bryn's voice raised an octave.

Eric smirked. "No. Not at all. I think he's a total freak show. But I do think there are things men can do that women can't and things women can do that men can't, and I accept that."

"What? Giving birth? Not all women can do that, you know." A little more venom than he expected spewed from her statement. Where was the heat coming from?

"Bryn, I do not think men are superior to women. You know me, right?"

Bryn sighed. "Yeah. I'm just rubbed the wrong way and tired."

Eric pulled into the church parking lot.

"Why are we here?"

"Were you not listening? I have to talk to Patty and get some forms for camp. I'll be a few. Come on in with me. Stretch your legs."

Bryn climbed from the SUV. "You still work as a boys' counselor for Royal Family Kids' Camp?"

"Yep." This camp, led through his church, had changed his life. Helping abused and neglected children realize God's love and good plan for them was a message he'd never get tired of delivering. Connecting with the kids for a week to show them that they were safe and cared for was a highlight of his year. Took vacation for it.

"Still want a houseful of kiddos?" she asked quietly.

"One hundred percent yes. The world needs half a dozen little Eric and Erica Hales running around making their humorous mark on the world." He nudged her, but she bristled. "Don't let this guy and his warped sense of the sexes jack you up. We're gonna get him. And you can lay the cuffs on him. Show him who's the real man."

"That was sexist."

"That was a joke. I like it when you smile." Eric opened the door for her and followed her inside the lobby. He loved the smell of church—lemon, coffee and holiness.

Eric held the glass door to the inner offices open for Bryn. Harriet, the secretary, beamed. He smiled and waved but spoke to Bryn. "See, would a sexist jerk hold a door open for you?"

"I guess not. Unless he was planning on stabbing me in the back or jabbing an ice pick into my skull."

"Fair enough. But I'd think I'd want to see your face when I took you down. Totally ride the wave of scaring you half to death."

"To death. No halfsies."

"Good point. Hi, Harriet," Eric said and breezed past her, working not to laugh at her ashen face and quizzical expression. Ah, the things you could talk about with a fellow law enforcer without being looked on as a morbid freak.

Patty, a social worker in her midfifties, sat at a desk in the office workstation area putting together packets for camp.

"Hey, Pats. You remember Bryn Eastman. It's been a few years."

Patty's eyebrows rose, but she smiled. "Of course. Can't forget a woman this pretty." She stood and shook Bryn's hand. "Good to see you again. How've you been?"

"Well, thank you."

"Good." She handed Eric the paperwork. "A list of our meetings is on the back page so you can schedule around them best you can."

"Great. June. Gives me plenty of time to put in my vacation request. You need anything else?"

Patty shook her head. "No. I saw Angela this morning. I'm taking her to the health department tomorrow for aid and an examination."

Eric rolled his papers up like a tube. "How'd she seem to you?"

"Tired. Scared. We'll get her through it. She's keeping the baby." Patty sighed. "I'll be honest, I think adoption is a better decision at this point, but a lot can happen in five months. She could clean up and be a suitable parent."

Eric pictured Angela's child at the Royal Family Kids' Camp by the time he or she turned five. Broke his heart. "Keep me posted, and let me know if she needs anything else. Oh, wait." He dug into his pocket, pulled out his wallet and dropped three one-hundred-dollar bills in Patty's hand. "Make sure she's fed and clothed. If you need more, holler."

Patty's eyes filled with moisture. "I'm so proud of you. Thank you."

"I'm not doing it for you to feel proud, but you're welcome." Taking a compliment felt prideful and selfish, but Patty hadn't meant it to flatter him. He was doing better at simply saying "thank you."

"It was nice to see you again, Bryn. We could use a few more female counselors, if you're around and interested. First week of June. We'd love to have you."

Bryn's face turned pink. "Oh, um...thank you for offering. I'll—I'll think about it." Bryn had always talked about working a camp with him. Unfortunately, it had always coincided with her swim meets. No asking for time off when you were on a scholarship. But she'd never shied away from the idea like now. Guess she thought it would be awkward. He'd love to share the experience with her, though.

He had to quit thinking like that.

Everything surrounding this case was dangerous. From

Bryn's threats and attacks to the way Eric's heart longed to have more than it could.

Time to focus on the case alone. "How about we make a little trip to see Julian Proctor?"

Bryn's shoulders relaxed. "Yeah, let's do that."

As if anything sounded better than discussing camp and working alongside him personally.

EIGHT

Lunch had been quiet. Bryn wasn't in a talkative mood. Not after Patty's invitation to help out with the kids' camp, something she'd wanted to be a part of—with Eric. Back when she'd dreamed of being a swim coach and raising brown-eyed children like their father—children who inherited his humor and swam like fish.

So much for her dreams.

After the semi-silent lunch, Eric had made a call to Baptist Memorial Hospital to see if Julian Proctor was working. He wasn't. So they'd driven to his luxury home only to find out from a nosy neighbor that he spent most of his time on the golf course. During the conversation with the elderly woman, Bryn had zoned out again and missed part of the discussion; it was becoming a habit she couldn't afford.

At the stoplight Eric shifted toward her. "You've got the I-can't-find-the-coffee-canister face again."

She ignored his subtle prying. Her issues were none of his business, especially since part of her problem was him. "Well, *you* look disgusted. What's your deal?"

Eric groaned. "Edgewood. That's my dad's golf club."

Fantastic. Just what she needed, another physical reminder they could never be together. Bryn had never felt welcome around Brooks Hale. If she had to guess, he never thought Bryn was good enough for his son. She came from middle-class, blue-collar workers and lived in a one-story, three-bedroom home. If not for her swim scholarship, she might not have made it to college. Who knew?

"So, golf course or bust?"

She was already about to bust.

Bringing up Dad had zipped Bryn's lips. But then she'd been distant since the episode with Patty. On the drive to Edgewood, Eric had been thinking about the approach. "I know you're all FBI, but I think I should go in alone and talk to Proctor. If he's there."

Bryn bristled. "Because he hates women?"

"There's that." And the fact Dad was probably having a before-dinner drink with his friends, and bringing Bryn in wouldn't be a stellar move. And also… "Not to add fuel to the fire, but do you know why I dislike this club so much?"

"Because it reminds you of your dad guilting you into golf and manipulating you to keep doing it. And showing you off as a trophy to his friends rather than treating you as a beloved son."

Eric clenched his jaw. "Again, there's…that."

Bryn's eyes widened. "I'm sorry. That was out of line."

But it was true. "This was an exclusive men's golf club until legislation said it was discriminating. The mind-set remains, and while they've included women and other ethnic backgrounds, it continues to be exclusively white men who think they're hot snot."

Bryn smirked.

"Yeah, I said 'hot snot.'" He laid a hand on her shoulder and gave her a playful push, hoping to shake off her melancholy. "They built a small women's area. I don't even know how many women actually are members. That's not public information, but I can tell you that they're snubbed. Would you want to be a member where you knew deep down you weren't wanted?"

"Your dad's against gender equality?"

"He's for male bonding over brandy, cigars and golf. He's for making business deals in a plush leather chair with a roaring fireplace and using seedy language without feeling the need to apologize."

Bryn grunted. "I thought your family attended church."

"They do. Every Sunday. But church doesn't change you. Does look good to the community, though." Eric wished Dad and Mom would have more of a relationship with God. It would help them grieve and bring them comfort if they would open up and let God heal them. It's how Eric had healed and forgiven Bryn, although she wasn't to blame in the first place.

It was Rand's fault. And the evil that resided in his heart. Like cold black ice.

Just like the killer they were tracking. Clearly, Julian Proctor was filled with hate, and hate was inspired and bred by nothing more than evil in its coldest form.

"I don't care. I'm going in. I'm not going to cower in the car because I don't have a Y chromosome." She set her jaw, her stare confident and unchanging.

No point arguing. Bryn wasn't going to see reason. "Fine, but if I say some things that are slightly discriminatory toward your gender, know it's an act."

"Fine."

Bryn had trouble concentrating at times. "Repeat back to me what I said."

Bryn snorted. "I will not."

Eric turned into the elite Edgewood Golf Club. Golf carts driven by caddies carried wealthy businessmen to the course. If the large white brick clubhouse with walled windows and ornate carved wooden doors had a nose, it'd be stuck right up in the air like most of the members'.

"But you did hear me, right?"

Bryn flipped the mirror down and fiddled with her hair.

"Yes. You're going to act like a pig in order to gain some ground with these Neanderthals, and then you're going to schmooze with them so they'll talk to you."

"In a nutshell."

"Fine, but no blonde jokes, Hale. I mean it." A twitch at her lip said she agreed with his strategy.

"Fine. You take the lead at the moment."

"Why? So you can bust in and 'put me in my place'?"

He paused at the door and leaned down to her ear. "If I could put you in your place, you'd have someone spending the night at your house every single night." The scent of oranges and vanilla dizzied him. "Now open the door. I don't want to come across as a gentleman."

She breathed a laugh and opened the door into the clubhouse.

The floral scent from the monstrous vase atop a round mahogany table in the middle of the foyer mingled with faint cigar smoke and chlorine. To the right, French doors opened to a dining room. They approached the rounded desk. "Edgewood Golf Club" scrolled in gold screamed elite.

The man behind the counter smiled at Eric. "May I help you, sir?" He glanced at Bryn. "Ma'am."

Bryn's jaw tightened.

Eric stepped forward. "I'm Eric Hale."

The man's eyes widened. "Oh, my apologies. I didn't recognize you without your golf clubs." His eyes slid toward Bryn again. "Will you be playing with a…friend?"

"Not today. I'm looking for—"

"Me?" Dad's voice echoed through the empty foyer, pinging off every single glass dome on the chandelier, it seemed. Eric had hoped he wouldn't run into Dad today, at least not with Bryn in tow.

He turned as Bryn did.

Dad's steely-gray eyes met Bryn's blue-greens. "What

are you doing here?" He cast a glare toward Eric. "I thought I made it crystal clear that I didn't want to see her face. Ever. Period."

Bryn squared her shoulders and glared with cool eyes. Eric was proud of her brave front, but her chin quivered, if only for a second. He stepped in front of her, shielding Bryn from his father.

"You're crossing a line, Dad."

"I know the SAC at the bureau. Maybe you won't have to work with her much longer."

"Now isn't the time for this. We're working a case."

"Here? Ha!"

Bryn stepped around Eric, shot him a dirty look and faced the larger-than-life Brooks Hale. "You can call in every favor in the book. But SAC Towerman won't change his mind about this case. He practically begged me to take it." She inched closer to Dad. "Because there's nobody better than me when it comes to catching killers. I've had homegrown training. I'm even better than your son. So why don't you sport on out with those hideous pants and arrogant swagger, and play the back nine while we stop a man from murdering Memphis women." With that, she wheeled around and stalked past the dining room toward the back of the club.

"Ma'am, I'll need you to—"

Whirling around, Bryn flashed her credentials. "That's all you need."

Eric didn't miss her expression. Raw anger mixed with deep hurt. He wiped his hand across his face.

"How dare she!" Dad's jaw worked in tandem with his nostril flares.

"How dare *she*? She's a person. With feelings. And she didn't murder Abby. She didn't even drive her away with insurmountable pressure to be something she wasn't. *You* did that. You did it to the both of us."

"You think I drove Abby to self-medicate?"

Eric almost snorted. *Self-medicate* was a fancy word for drug use. But Brooks Hale would never admit his daughter had been doing just that, or was even beginning to fall into that cycle. All Eric's work to mend his relationship with his father over the past few years was falling apart. It'd been eggshells to begin with, and this moment cracked the shell, sending the yolks and whites splattering to the ground.

"Stop defending her. Are you…seeing her on the side?"

As if Bryn were someone he'd need to sneak to see. "I'm not defending her. And if I was, it's my business and you'd have to deal with it."

"I can't believe you'd do this to your mother. I'm disappointed in you, Eric."

What was new? "And I'm disappointed in you." Their relationship just fried on the pan of their heated words. Or in this case, considering where he was, it had just been poached.

Dad raised a silvery eyebrow and turned his regal form, calmly ambling away as if Eric had just agreed to have a steak with him. Not even an ounce of remorse for his hurtful words. Raking his hands through his hair, Eric turned to the man at the desk who had conveniently disappeared. *Great.*

Now to find Bryn. See if there was any way to make this right. Sadly, words couldn't be taken back. You couldn't unhear something. Not that she hadn't known of Dad's hatred for her. Hopefully, Bryn wouldn't hold it against Eric. Like he didn't hold Rand's actions against her.

He stalked into the dining area. Where would she have gone? With her emotions like a loose cannon, who knew what she'd do when she found Julian Proctor. Did Dad know Julian? Were they friends? The thought sickened him. While hunting for Bryn, he made sure to keep an eye out for the creepy doctor.

He exited the dining hall onto the terrace that led to an outdoor courtyard and pool. There sat Julian Proctor drinking what looked to be Scotch or bourbon, smoking a cigar and laughing with no doubt another complete jerk.

He was tall with a receding hairline connected by gray hairs and a few spots of pepper, revealing he'd been dark-haired in his youth. Eyes as black as a shark's connected with Eric's.

Time to reel in this woman hater. See if he'd cough up his connection with Rusty Beckham on his own. If so, he might not have anything to hide other than being a misogynist.

"Julian Proctor?" Eric held up his shield. "I'm Detective Eric Hale."

"Ah," Julian said. "Brooks's son. I've seen you on the course." He held his hand out to shake. "Good to meet you."

Eric begrudgingly shook his hand.

"My game's been off. Might need to hire you for lessons." Julian grinned, and the man across from him chuckled.

"Another time." As in never. "I'd like to ask you a few questions if that's okay." *Play nice. Keep your disgust from showing, Eric.*

The man across the table stood. "We'll pick up later, Julian. Enjoy the bourbon."

Julian saluted with his drink and returned his attention to Eric.

"I'd like to talk to you about your coalition. M.A.G.E."

Julian used his hand to offer Eric a seat. "What would you like to know? Interested in joining?"

Eric grinned. "Maybe. My partner is a female, and she's really starting to wear me thin."

Julian sipped his bourbon. "What do you really want to talk about, Detective?"

"Do you know Rusty Beckham?" Eric studied Julian's face. Not so much as a twitch of the eyes.

"Should I?"

No admission either way. *Clever. Crafty man.* In case Proctor was feeling him out to see what he knew, Eric kept the bail card in his pocket. For now. "We found a newsletter in his apartment. We assume he's a member of your coalition." Eric leaned back, cocked a foot over his knee, not at all uncomfortable with his surroundings. He'd cut his baby teeth on the golf course, in clubs like this. In this one.

"I have many members. I don't personally address the newsletters. What has this Rusty fellow done?" Amusement flickered in his eyes.

"He may have murdered four women, and he's threatened and physically attacked my partner."

"The female?" The way Julian said *female*, as if it were a vile word, sent a chill into Eric's blood.

"Yes."

"So you're here for her?"

"I'm here hoping you'll help me find a killer." Eric leaned across the table, met Julian's stare and held it. Mind games. Cryptic talk. Hiding that he'd bailed Rusty out of jail. This guy was guilty. "What company do you use for your lawn care?"

"Grass Is Greener."

"Rusty Beckham works for that company."

Julian finished his bourbon and set it down, ice clinking. He inhaled and pasted a smug smile on his face, then he leaned forward an inch as if to share a dark and delightful secret with Eric. "Mowing my grass won't get you anything but a laugh from a judge or a jury." He knew Eric was trying to connect them. And he didn't care. A smart guy like him would surely know a detective had done his research before asking questions. Why not admit to knowing Rusty?

Games. He was simply playing games.

"No, but you bailed him out of jail. So that might. Do you typically do that for strangers?"

Julian held Eric's gaze; his cheek twitched. "Rusty Beckham is an embarrassment. In order to keep my coalition and reputation in good standing, I bailed him out. I don't appreciate overzealous members using violence in my name. And if you dig deep enough, you'll also see that I paid the man Rusty assaulted to drop the charges. You can see how that would look bad on me, right? I don't believe in violence." A smirk played around his lips. "I'm a law-abiding citizen."

Eric clenched his jaw, working to keep calm.

"Maybe you should have stuck with golf." A deep chuckle rumbled in Julian's throat.

Eric pulled a slip of paper from his pocket. "I'd like to know where you were on these dates." Days the victims went missing. Eric slid them over to Julian.

He perused them, then reached into his wallet and handed Eric a card. "This is my attorney. You want to see my schedule, get a warrant." He pushed the paper back to Eric. "And Detective Hale, I'd be careful, you and that towheaded female partner of yours." He stood. "You don't want to find yourself with a harassment suit from someone like me." He took his time taking the concrete stairs toward the pool area, then he disappeared behind another row of French doors.

Eric leaned back and breathed deep. Who did this guy think he was? He all but dared them to keep coming. And then he made an indirect threat against him and Bryn.

Wait…*towheaded*. How did he know she was blonde? She had gone in the opposite direction when she'd stormed off. And there was no way Proctor could have seen them come in.

His senses went on high alert. He had to find her. Wherever she was.

And now.

NINE

Bryn's hand trembled. Inside, it was as if someone had turned on a jackhammer and let it loose. Anger. Pain. Fear. Humiliation. She hadn't fooled herself into believing the Hale family had forgiven her. She'd been surprised that Eric had. But the words... They were anguish to her soul. It wasn't her fault, and it had taken time for her to see that.

Her cheeks had ballooned with heat and still burned. Eric had stood in front of her, as if she couldn't fight her own battle. That had seriously rankled. By doing that, he gave the impression she was frail. Unable to handle Brooks Hale.

But she had handled him. And claiming her dignity had felt good.

Now she wandered through the women's gym to the pool. Empty. Just as Eric said it would be. She inhaled the chlorine scent as she stared at the quiet water. Sunlight streaked in through the wall of windows, filling the room with its golden warmth. What she wouldn't give to jump in and swim until she was fatigued and her stress was relieved.

Squatting, she ran her fingertips over the silent water, creating ripples. Raising her hand, she let the water droplets ping back into the pool where they belonged. She wanted to belong to Eric. After the display in the lobby, it was abundantly clear that would never happen.

Wiping her wet hands on her pants, she entered the women's locker room to use the restroom. The male members here might turn their noses up at female members, but they'd spared no expense on the locker room. Damp but pristine. White tiled floors and matching changing stalls, individual showers and curtains. She slipped into a stall, then exited and washed her hands.

Suddenly, a chill spiked the hairs on her arms and neck. As if something or someone had entered the unoccupied space. She left the water running in the sink and stood statue-still, listening for footsteps.

Pivoting quietly, she drew her weapon, her breath shallow. Sweat beaded on her upper lip, but her arm stayed steady as her training kicked in. Edging around a section of metal lockers, she whipped right, her gun pointing on the aisle before her.

Clear.

Was her imagination wreaking havoc with her? With everything she'd endured in the past year and especially the past couple of weeks, it wouldn't surprise her. Keeping her back to the lockers, she inched down another row and cleared the aisles until she'd been through all seven.

Straight ahead was the steam room; wisps of air slipped like fog from one of the cracked double doors.

She swallowed and trained her gun on the opening.

Might as well clear it and give her mind some peace. The sense of being watched heightened; her pulse pounded at her temples.

Using her foot, she kicked the white towel obstructing the door from closing, and stretched it open farther. Steam poured out, blurring her vision.

"FBI, anyone in there?"

Nothing but the sound of the water running in the sink on the other side of the room and the hiss of steam.

She stepped inside, glued her back to the wall. Double

rows of wooden benches stretched across two walls and a few towels had been left inside. She released a pent-up breath.

The sound of the door opening had her swinging around. She pointed her weapon at her attacker.

"Whoa!" Eric raised his hands. "Put that thing away. You didn't hear me call out for you? For anyone?"

Bryn nearly collapsed on a bench. She was losing it, creating prowlers around every corner. Frightening memories and the latest attempts on her life fueling her imagination.

"Sorry." She holstered her weapon. "No. Was there? Anyone in here?"

Eric closed the distance between them, the door slowly shutting again. "No. It's empty. Just water running from a sink. What are you doing in here? It's hot as all get out."

"Said the man who wants to move to Florida." She wiped a bead of sweat from her forehead. "I thought someone might be in here. I'm jumpy, to put it mildly."

"You have good reason. I'm jumpy myself."

Bryn forced a smile. "Let's get out of this place. It's too hot."

"Mmm. And my Twizzlers might melt." Eric took her hand, but she jerked away.

"Did you hear that?" Bryn whispered. "Sounded like someone is at the door."

Eric returned the whisper. "No." Neither moved. Bryn heard Eric's gun slip from his holster. If he didn't hear anything, why draw his weapon?

A sound of metal scraping at the fogged door made Bryn jump. "That noise," Bryn hissed.

Eric grabbed the handle and pushed. "It's—it's jammed." He rammed his shoulder into it repeatedly.

Steam shot from the top vents. "Eric, can you control the steam level from in here?"

Eric rammed the door again. "No. It's set on a timer, but you can adjust it manually…on the outside."

Bryn reached for her phone. No signal. "My cell won't work! Try yours. We can call the front desk to come get us out."

Eric sighed. "No can do. They don't allow cell phones in the locker room. Pervs and pics and all. They scramble the signal in case someone doesn't adhere to the rules. My phone won't work, either."

"What happens if it gets cranked and we can't get out?" Bryn's stomach quivered.

"I don't want to find out."

But they might have to. Someone had locked them in and turned up the heat. Someone who might know too much steam and humidity could do dangerous things to their bodies. Dehydration for one.

Someone like a doctor.

"Do you think Julian Proctor is in the clubhouse?"

"No." Eric slammed his shoulder into the doors again, then shook out of his jacket and tried again. "I *know* he is. I talked to him."

Steam continued to consume the room until Eric's hazy face was completely covered. Nothing but humid air suffocating them. Bryn shucked out of her coat. "Can we shoot our way out?"

"Do you want to risk a bullet ricocheting in this sweat-box? Not to mention going deaf."

The thought of a bullet ripping through her flesh, again, sent a wave of nauseous shivers through her body. She bent at the knees. "We have to get out of here."

"Aware of that." Eric banged on the door and hollered for help.

"Give up. I didn't hear you calling my name. No one is going to hear your call for help unless they're standing at the door. Besides, it's clear the women's area is empty."

Eric muttered under his breath. "When we get out of here, I'm going to personally put my fist through the doctor's face."

"What did he say?" Bryn joined Eric ramming the door. "When you talked to him." Sweat slicked down her back like sheets of water, her hair matted to her neck and her pants glued to her legs. "Isn't there a manual button or emergency switch that will open the door?"

Eric began feeling along the far wall. Bryn took the opposite side.

"He says he doesn't personally know Rusty Beckham, just bailed him out to avoid a tainted reputation, but he admitted to using Grass Is Greener. Then he basically told me I had squat and to go back to golfing."

"I'm not buying that. They're in this together. Somehow." Bryn met Eric in the middle. No emergency button.

Eric felt her face like a blind man, sliding her hair from her cheek and tucking it behind her ears. "We'll get out of here."

"How can you stay so calm?" Bryn's blood whooshed in her ears, but his soothing tone relaxed and gave her hope.

"Because I'd never let anything happen to you, Bryn. And I'm sorry about my father. That you had to hear that."

So was she. But she wasn't going to apologize for her outburst. "If someone doesn't come, we're in trouble. We may have to risk putting a bullet through the door."

She pushed on the handles, turned her body into a battle-ax and went to work on breaking down the door. Eric's hand rested on Bryn's soaked shoulder. "You know you're right. You are better than me."

"What?" Bryn's head had turned fuzzy. "Better than…" It dawned. She had told Eric's dad that. "I don't think that. I was mad at your dad." She pounded on the door and gave up. It was no use. They were going to dehydrate, and then who knew what it might do to their oxygen levels. "I'm sweating bullets here." *God, please get us out of here. I know I've not been speaking much...okay at all to You. But if not for me for Eric.*

"I know it's not the time or place, but I'm proud of you and who you've become, Bryn. I don't think the old Bryn would have ever stood up to Brooks Hale."

Probably not. She had changed. Been forced to. "Well, thank you. You're really good at your job. I don't think I'm better. Honestly. I mostly wanted to tick off your dad."

The bench creaked. Eric had stood on it and was feeling around the ceiling. "Mission accomplished. He was thoroughly ticked."

Bryn sank onto the bench. "Eric, I'm light-headed."

"Well, you haven't had time to recover from the attack at the Grass Is Greener. Put your head between your knees and don't think of clear mountain streams."

Bryn did as he asked and thought of bubbling brooks. Alaskan glaciers. Her throat ached from dryness.

"Ha! A Jedi knows."

Bryn's head popped up. Or it looked like it did. "What? What does a Jedi know?"

"Are you admitting I'm a Jedi?" Bryn was on the edge, and if he lost his cool—irony right there—she'd wither. Whatever he had to do to keep her preoccupied, he'd do it, even if it meant tossing out movie references, picking at her to rile her up, teasing or flirting. But his stomach was wound tighter than a T-shirt during the spin cycle, and he was light-headed, as well. His shirt and jeans clung to him like a second skin. He was soaked through and willing to give up his entire inheritance for a drink of water. He'd never related to Esau in the Bible more in his whole life.

"I'd admit you were king if you know a way out."

"Okay, admit it, then." He pushed on the grate above him until it gave way and clattered to the floor.

"What was that?" Bryn stood and looked up. "Ventilation?"

"We're going up and out, babe."

Babe. He bit his tongue and regretted the endearment. It had slid out too easily. Bryn didn't acknowledge it. She climbed on the bench next to him.

"Okay, then."

"How do you feel?"

"Like I want to crawl out of here and stop these guys. If we don't, who knows what they'll do next."

Eric was afraid to find out. "We will. It's a jump, so…" He placed his hands on her waist. The fact that she was covered in sweat didn't stop his heart from pounding harder or the zip of awareness in the air between them.

Her breath released in a clipped pant. From the lack of air or from his touch? Couldn't go there.

"On three, jump, and I'll boost you up."

Bryn turned, her nose inches from his. Even with the sweat, she smelled like an orange Creamsicle. Up close, through the steam, he watched as her eyes trekked to his lips, as she bit her own and then made eye contact with him. "This is the fourth time you've saved my life."

What he would give to kiss her. His inheritance. Forget the water. He wanted to drink her in. All her warmth, her goodness and kindness. Her sincerity. "Well," his voice erupted huskier than he wanted, "let's see where that duct leads us."

They stood gazing at each other, a moment passing between them he couldn't quite put a finger on. Didn't want to. If they weren't about to melt, he'd stay here this way forever. "Ready?" he breathed.

She nodded and swiveled back around. On three, she

jumped, and he lifted her into the ductwork. Didn't take too much effort; Bryn had powerful swimmer's legs.

When she was in the duct, she hollered, "I can't see anything, but there's room for you."

Eric hoisted himself up and fidgeted in his pocket for the tiny flashlight he kept. He switched it on. "You're taking the lead. Here."

He shimmied and wiggled his way through the ventilation, following Bryn. "I don't see any grates to knock out so we can swing into open space. Left or right?"

"You want to flip a coin?"

"What happened to your Jedi sense?"

He laughed. "That's um, Spidey sense, Bryn. For as many TV shows and movies as you watch, you don't quite know your facts."

"Right it is." Bryn shifted right.

Eric followed suit. It wasn't exactly cool in the ducts, but it was better than the steamy humidity. "You know we can't prove Julian locked us in the steam room. And whatever he used to jam us in there will doubtfully have prints."

"Don't remind me. I've already thought of that. Grate!" Bryn punched it until it fell into the floor. She dropped below, and Eric edged over the open space, then copied her.

They stood in a storage locker full of towels and sports equipment. "Cozy," Eric said.

Bryn shook her head, unlocked the door and turned the knob. She laid her head on the door and groaned.

"What?" Eric turned the knob. Must be padlocked from the outside. "Seriously. You broke us out to lock us in a storage facility?"

Bryn peered up at the grate. "I cannot believe this."

Eric's muscles ached. He wanted a cold drink and a cold shower. Instead, he grabbed a towel and dried his soaking head, face and neck. Bryn snatched one and did the same.

A clank came from the other side of the door, then a click sounded and it opened.

A college-age dude stood, mouth hanging open, padlock in hand. "How did you get—what are you doing in here?"

Eric took Bryn's towel and handed both to the kid. "You were out of towels in the locker room." He strode past the guy, and Bryn fell into step with him.

They were free for the moment but not out of the woods yet. Someone wanted Bryn dead and maybe even him now. He hadn't taken Julian's words lightly.

"Let's get crime techs out here to dust that door for prints and figure out how we got locked inside."

"Can we get something to drink first?" Bryn smirked as they walked through the halls, members gawking at their sweat-drenched clothing.

"Absolutely." He slipped in the lounge, grabbed two waters from the cooler, came out and tossed her one. They entered the locker room and waited on the techs to remove the barbell—with two hundred pounds of weights screwed onto the ends—that had been wedged between the two metal door handles. By the time they reached the Durango, they'd sucked down two bottles of water apiece.

They hadn't tracked down Julian Proctor because Edgewood kept all things private. No video cameras. Not even in the parking lot. No evidence.

The biting wind was a burst of relief on his hot skin, but soon it turned to chill bumps, leaving a film like after a good workout. On the way to Bryn's, neither spoke much. He turned into her drive. Holt's car wasn't there. "You're not going in alone."

"I don't really want to if I'm being honest."

Eric was scared to death to let her leave. "I'll help you clear the house and come back after I shower. You wanna grab dinner?"

Bryn rubbed her lips together and averted her gaze.

"I—I don't think so. Not tonight. I appreciate you clearing the house, and if you want to send an unmarked car… I'd be grateful. Or I can call one in myself."

Dad's words had made a direct hit on Bryn's heart. Eric wanted to pummel the wheel. But maybe a night apart to think through things was wise. "I can do it. I'll do it now." He made the call while they sat inside the car.

Bryn grabbed her purse. "I…"

What? Something flashed in her eyes, and he desperately wanted to hear her say it didn't matter what his dad thought. That after today she'd realized she hadn't stopped caring about him, hadn't stopped loving him. But instead she shook her head and climbed out of the car.

At the front door, she pulled her gun. "You don't think this might be a little absurd?"

"We were almost steamed to death. I now know what broccoli feels like."

Bryn didn't laugh, but she nodded and let out a whoosh of air as she entered the house. "Clear." Newton barked and clawed at the puppy gate penning him into the kitchen. "Just a minute, little guy."

Eric finished the living room and kitchen. "Clear."

Bryn entered her bedroom and bathroom. "Clear."

"You check under the bed?" Eric asked.

Bryn snorted. "You serious?"

Eric checked under her bed. "Clear-ish. What is all that junk under there?"

"I have no idea."

"I'm going to clear the garage."

Bryn was already opening the back door to let the pooch out. When Eric came back in, he sat at the kitchen table. "I'm not staying. Just waiting on you to get the dog back inside and lock the door."

"I'm safe now. It'll be okay. Plus the unmarked car will be here soon." She didn't appear too convinced. "Go home and peel out of those clothes, take a shower and crawl into bed. That's what I plan to do."

"Well, can I get a drink of water first? My throat is still dry."

Bryn scratched Newton's ears. "Bottles in the fridge."

Eric opened the fridge and grabbed a couple. "Get some rest, okay?"

She gave a tight smile. "Sure."

"You need anything, call me." He hesitated leaving her. But the extra measure of security would be here soon. "Keep your gun on you. I don't like leaving, Bryn. Too much has happened. I'm sick over walking out that door."

"I know. The house is secure. I'll keep my gun. And I'll call you if I need you. I promise."

"Not after the fact." He silently prayed there wouldn't be an after-the-fact reason to call.

"I promise." Bryn walked him to the door.

Outside, his phone rang.

Angela.

"Hey, Ang."

"I made a mistake. I'm sorry. I shouldn't have texted him back but…"

Eric glanced down at his damp clothes and sighed. "I'm on my way. Hang tight."

TEN

Bryn stood in front of Dr. Warner's tank, watching tropical fish swim without a care in the world. Some of the smaller fish darted in and out of the pirate ship as if playing tag.

Dr. Warner sat on the couch wearing charcoal-gray slacks, a black button-down shirt—starched and ironed, rolled to his elbows—a smile on his face and every auburn hair in place.

She'd updated him on the case and what happened at the golf club—only because he'd know it anyway from the reports—but she'd revealed nothing personal. She'd told him she'd do better. This wasn't better. Bryn had been failing. The killer stayed a step ahead of her and continued to terrorize and attack her. She wasn't sure how long she could keep a brave exterior. Inside, she was crumbling. With every new assault, Ohio's nightmare crept back up from buried places. She continued to misplace things and forget. This couldn't go on much longer.

"I'd love to jump in that tank and swim with the fish. Just swim and swim and swim. It's so quiet under the water. Peaceful." Ironic thought since the victims had drowned. That wouldn't have been peaceful or quiet. Drowning was a violent death, one that would have been fought tooth and nail.

"I think you'd disrupt their environment."

"I met with SAC Towerman. I have to report to him every morning and each evening, as you're well aware," she muttered. Today's conversation had sent her over the edge. He'd shoved her into the field against what he called his better judgment. And now he wanted to pull her back and put in another agent. After all Bryn had done and accomplished, she deserved to see this through. But Dr. Warner's notes had obviously made it to Towerman's desk, and they hadn't been in her favor. So much for opening up to him. Clearly that hadn't worked.

"How do you feel about what he said?" Dr. Warner asked.

Could he not state his opinion? Even once? "What do you think? I have a lead. Which is more than anyone had before. I don't want to give it up now." Even if she had been attacked and threatened more than she'd made headway. "This guy has targeted me—staying in the field makes more sense. Bait." Not that she liked the idea of being bait. It terrified her, but this guy wasn't going to quit. He'd kill her if he could and continue to murder other women. He had to be stopped.

"Bait?" Dr. Warner's eyes held concern.

"Yes. He's a misogynistic miscreant." She gave the fish one more longing glance. Tonight she'd go to the gym and take a long therapeutic swim. A crowded gym with no steam room. "I can beat him. But not behind a desk." A desk wouldn't protect her from him anyway. Her stomach knotted again.

Bryn hadn't offered up much more than what Dr. Warner already knew. It was time to share some personal feelings with the hope that his next report wouldn't seal her future from the field. As they said: desperate times called for desperate measures.

Pinching the bridge of her nose, she shook her head. "The man I'm assisting, the lead homicide detective…"

Dr. Warner flipped through the case file. "Eric Hale?"

"Yes. We...had a relationship. Almost a decade ago. Before Rand killed his sister. She was his last victim."

Dr. Warner's eyebrows rose. "I see."

Bryn's chest squeezed. This wasn't easy, talking about Eric. "Some old feelings have surfaced along with some new ones. I'm not sure what to make of it all."

Dr. Warner sat silent.

"I'll admit, I'm stressed to the max. If you'd sign off on my full competence to be in the field, that'd help relieve some of it." She grinned.

He didn't.

Fine. "I might be misplacing things around the house and fighting to keep focused. But it's not affected my job and neither have these newly developed feelings for Eric."

Yet.

Dr. Warner uncrossed his ankle from over his knee and leaned forward. "That's not uncommon for a person with large amounts of stress, Agent Eastman. Is there anything on your plate you can scrape off?"

"Nothing comes to mind. I think it's more about all the things in my head not so much what I have to do."

"Like?"

Bryn swallowed the ball growing in her throat. She didn't want to discuss Eric further, but the truth was she was wrestling with the pain. The truth. "Eric wants a house full of kids." Tears stung the back of her eyes. "Dozens of Eric and Erica Hales leaving their brown-eyed marks on the world. I can't give him that anymore." Every second she spent with him, it weighed on her. "It doesn't matter, I suppose. We're never going to be together. What Rand did will always hang between us, and his parents detest me."

"And if you both could get past what your brother did? If his parents did forgive you? Then what?" Dr. Warner scribbled on his notepad. "Are you afraid he wouldn't understand? Wouldn't want you because you can't have children?" Of course he knew her situation. Had her medical file, as well as case files. But hearing someone else say it aloud...hurt.

Bryn covered her face with her hands. "No," she whispered. "He would. He'd probably be sickeningly supportive. But it wouldn't be fair. He deserves to have children. It's been his dream. It's why he has that big house. He'd end up resenting me."

Bryn had too much baggage, and it wasn't just dragging along behind her. It was dragging her down. She wanted to go back to that night. To be able to be a mom. To stop feeling scared. Stop having panic attacks, seeing Scott Mulhoney's face before she drifted off to sleep at night.

"How are you sleeping? Are you taking the sedatives?"

"Not every night but most. I sleep okay."

"Do you want something stronger?"

She shook her head. If she went into too deep of a sleep, she might not wake if someone tried to get into her house. A thought that horrified her, even if she did protest to having someone stay with her. She couldn't be a coward forever. There had to be a line between being petrified and concerned. Having a guard in her own home crossed that line. "I'll be okay with what I have."

"Our time is up for today. I'm glad you're talking, Agent Eastman. I think you'll find it does help. Before next Friday, you need to come up with a few things you can cut in order to gain control of your faculties. Like you said, too much crowding."

"But what?" What could she possibly remove from her life? She had no real friends. She worked, ate and slept.

Dr. Warner stood. "That's for you to figure out, Agent Eastman. I can't make that choice for you."

She couldn't ditch her puppy, the work on the rental house, this case. But Eric? If she could stop thinking about him and all the could-have-beens… How did one take control of their feelings for someone? Bryn had moved away, told herself every day that she needed to stop thinking about Eric and convinced herself she had moved on. Until she returned to Memphis and realized she hadn't.

Dr. Warner closed his office door behind him. "Friday at nine. Call if you need me before then."

Bryn made sure to use caution as she exited his office. Last time someone nearly left her riddled with a round of bullets. Nerves on end and hands clammy, she drew her weapon and surveyed the area as she made her way to her car, keeping to the shadows and making a wide berth around corners in case someone was lurking to grab her again.

When she cleared the area, she got into her car and rested her head on the back of the seat, relieved. Every muscle in her body ached from tension. When would this be over?

And how did one go about shutting off rising feelings for another person? She wasn't a robot.

Resolve.

Like when Daniel in the Bible refused to eat the king's food. He resolved in his heart not to defile himself. Not that Eric could be compared with King Nebuchadnezzar.

Eric was kind and charitable.

Helping Angela—who could have babies while Bryn couldn't.

She inhaled a cleansing breath and exhaled, resolving to guard her heart. This was a job and nothing more. No matter what, she would not let her heart dive into the pool and bask in the warm waters of Eric Hale.

"This is just a case. It's over between us. We have a friendship." Which might be too much for her to handle. If she continued easing into the waves of friendship, eventually her heart would drown. "We are colleagues. That's it."

Resolved. Done.

Then why did her chest fill with a dull ache?

* * *

Eric rubbed his eyes. Last night he'd gotten little sleep after Angela's call. She'd answered a text and told the baby's father where she was, and he showed up. With flowers and wine. Wine. She was pregnant! The jerk had tried to convince her to abort the baby, but she promised him that she'd keep him a secret and not ask for a dime.

The baby daddy didn't believe it. Eric couldn't blame him—he didn't believe it, either. Especially if he was as wealthy and elite in the city as Angela said he was. He got a little rough with her, and someone called security. He left before they showed up.

After harming her twice, she still refused to give Eric a name, which meant he couldn't pay him an official, or unofficial, visit. Couldn't arrest him. Nothing. Hands tied. Like he felt around Bryn. She had secrets, too.

She wasn't off her A-game, but she was overly distracted and occasionally missing out on bits of conversation, not to mention placing the coffee can with the dog food. And the hush-hush reason she'd been downtown. Plus, she'd been late to the office a couple of Fridays and refused to say why. Where was she going?

He filtered through the notes and reports her analyst had left them. Eric made a phone call and pulled Rusty's financials. Maybe he'd find some large financial deposits into his account in the last year. Of course, Julian was smart enough not to write a check. Money usually talked, though. Usually.

The door opened, and Bryn stepped inside. Cool. Calm. All business. Her eyes had a hard edge.

"We need to pull Rusty Beckham's financials. And Julian Proctor's."

"Just did that for Beckham," Eric responded. "We don't have probable cause to pull Julian's. The threat was indirect.

We didn't see him near the steam room. And him bailing out Rusty isn't enough."

"Well, let's get the members list from the coalition. Pull past rallies and see if we can put Rusty at one of those meetings."

Eric slowly turned in her direction. "We can connect them. We don't need eyewitnesses from the rallies to do that."

Bryn halted and squeezed the bridge of her nose. "Right. I—I don't know what I was thinking. Still, get them anyway. Maybe we can round up a witness overhearing them talk about one of the victims or something that might give us more to go on." Her clipped voice gave him pause. Had he done something to anger her? Irritate her at the very least?

"Okay, but we'll probably need to get a warrant. Which I think is doable knowing they are connected and Rusty beat up a guy who supported gender equality. But the list could have hundreds of members. That's a lot of people to comb through."

Something had happened again. Or she was hiding something new. Right now, she wasn't thinking clearly. Bryn was sharp, insightful and on top of the law. How had he never realized what an amazing law enforcer she'd be? It was obvious she was born to do this, but without the tragedy, Bryn most likely would be coaching a high school girls' swim team and diving in the Atlantic.

Bryn frowned. "Hundreds? I certainly hope not. There can't be that many stupid people out there."

Eric harrumphed. "Have you been out there?"

"I'm not going to allow this guy to slide by. Let's see *him* sweat for a change."

"I like that idea. I had to stay funky a lot longer than I planned. Thanks to Angela."

Bryn nabbed a file folder and sat beside Eric. "She show

up at your house? She and the baby all right?" Worry etched lines on her forehead.

Eric explained what happened.

Bryn closed the file. "When will she get into that unwed mother's home? The longer she stays isolated in a hotel, the worse it'll get. What if he comes back?"

"I moved her. To yet another hotel. But I can't take her phone from her or tie her to the chair." He wished he could. "Patty says they'll be able to get her into the home this coming Tuesday. They only have so many beds."

Bryn poked her lips out, her brow crinkled.

"Whacha thinking?"

Bryn shrugged. "How do you resolve something in your heart? How do you get mind over matter?"

Eric wasn't sure where this was going. "I don't know. What are you trying to resolve?"

She stood and paced the floor. "Nothing. I've got to paint the living room tonight."

Okay, left field. "Are you resolving that you want to paint?" He chuckled, but she didn't respond, just paced the floor fidgeting with her hands.

"Bryn, talk to me. You can trust me with whatever it is." Why wouldn't she just lay it all out there? Once she'd been open about everything. He knew her dreams and desires for life—to be a wife, a mom, a swim coach. Guess she could still dive and rescue whales and dolphins from fishermen's nets on the side, but it didn't look like she had. Instead, she worked to save people's lives.

She used to want a big flower garden and pool. He'd bought the house. Had the pool installed. He never used it. It was never for him.

With a sigh, she flicked her hand in the air, batting the conversation away. "I'm fine. I just need more sleep, I guess. I don't know." She stood in front of the board staring at the victims. "How does this guy grab these women without a struggle? That bugs me."

"Like you said. They know their lawn guy."

"No. After really studying them…they wouldn't have gone with Rusty willingly."

Someone knocked on the door. Percy came inside, his reddish-gold hair a thick disaster on his head. Blue eyes—small but bright—smiled. "I got that information you requested on the mayor and his wife."

"Great." Bryn snatched it and started reading.

"You still like him for it after all that's happened?" Eric stood behind her, reading over her shoulder. She shivered.

"Well look at that. Turns out Kaye McLoud did pay a little visit to Annalise Hemingway."

"Wonder why she backed out of the divorce."

Bryn pointed at the page. "If the dates are right, maybe because Annalise Hemingway was murdered before she could put her on retainer."

The mayor. A knot formed in Eric's gut. "Let's think this through, Bryn, before we go barging into his office with accusations. Rusty Beckham attacked you. Repeatedly. Julian Proctor locked us in the steam room, though we can't corroborate it. Beckham connects to all the victims and to Proctor. How does the mayor fit in?"

Bryn rubbed her face. "I don't know."

She had to see that the mayor wasn't a good option. "I think we need to keep him in our peripheral view but focus on making a solid case against Julian Proctor and Rusty Beckham. I also think we need to *find* Rusty Beckham." No prints on the notes. And ballistics got them nothing other than the make and model of the rifle. "We should put a tail on Proctor. See if he leads us to Beckham."

"He's too smart for that." Bryn tapped her chin with her index finger. "Maybe the mayor is connected but not in an I-offed-her kind of way."

"If we can connect the women to Julian Proctor, that would be a great help in securing a warrant. Did Bridgette Danforth ever protest him or the organization on her morning show?"

"It's worth checking into. I'll get Percy on it. But I doubt we'll connect them to Proctor like we did to Rusty. Each woman had public influence and ran in the same circles Julian Proctor runs in. All he'd need is to see them and fixate."

"Good point." Eric's stomach growled. "You hungry?"

"Not really."

It killed him to see her flustered, especially if he had anything to do with it. "Bryn, is what my dad said still eating at you?"

Bryn shook her head. "I expected as much. I admit a little part of me hoped he forgave me, since you and he reconciled your relationship."

"*Reconciled* is a relative term. I don't know if I'll ever have the kind of connection I want with him. Things have always been easier with Mom. You know that, although I use the word *easier* loosely."

"Family is important, and I hate that I'm the wedge even if it's just in name."

It wasn't Bryn's name that was a wedge. It was Eric's heart. How could he tell her that? He couldn't. "You're not to blame for anything."

"Even without Rand in the equation, they never thought I was good enough for you." She tucked some hair behind her ear.

Eric closed the distance between them and grasped her shoulders. "They don't think anyone is good enough for them, including me. I chose you." He wanted to choose her again. Mom and her failing heart sprang to mind. The fact Bryn might not feel the same way flashed next. He didn't see how they could make it work.

"Rand and I do have the same blood coursing through

our veins. I'm sure your family thinks deep down I'm just like him."

"You have entirely different hearts filtering and pumping it." He'd loved Bryn's heart, her ability to persevere, her dedication and loyalty to the things she loved—including him. "My dad is a bitter man. Bitter long before you ever came into the picture. So if that's what's got you all in a wad, please let it go."

She sucked her lip between her teeth and avoided eye contact with him. "We should probably focus on our job anyway."

It was getting harder each second.

The killer was out there. Focus was needed more than ever. Before he struck again.

And he would.

ELEVEN

Eric left Bryn's uneasy. She wasn't herself. The attacks weren't just taking their toll on her brain, although that might be a possible issue. He'd followed her home to let her dog out, which she argued about, but Eric didn't care. Later he'd help her clear her house and walk the dog, and then an unmarked car would show up if Holt couldn't be there.

But even at lunch earlier, she'd been frazzled and mentioned her coffeepot and cup were clean but she hadn't washed them. It bothered her more than it should. Eric did things on autopilot all the time, but he'd made a sweep of her house and didn't find any unlocked points of entry. And why would someone sneak in and do her dishes? That shouldn't worry her. She should be thankful. He had a sink full at his house. Whatever caused her to be late today had her in a tizzy. And all that talk of resolving issues.

Rusty was still out there, and a few days had gone by without any attacks. Eric's worry was warranted. What if this guy was planning a major attack? Eric circled city hall's parking lot. Bryn hadn't beat him here. She'd refused to ride together. Said she had somewhere to be after the interview, but Eric had a sneaky feeling she simply wanted some distance from him.

Inside he waited for about five minutes before Bryn breezed in, but her focus seemed to be elsewhere. City hall was a hubbub of busy people. Eric and Bryn sat in the mayor's office on his red plush couch, a coffee tray in front of them. The door opened and Mayor McLoud entered with his chief administrative officer, John Linden. A head taller than the gray-haired mayor, and two decades younger, the politician exuded power from the expensive suit to the flashy smile and perfect hair.

"Agent Eastman, Detective Hale, how can I be of service to you?" The mayor shook their hands, followed by another round with the CAO. They seated themselves across from Eric and Bryn. "Coffee?"

"No, thank you," Bryn said.

Eric's skin crawled at the way Linden's eyes roamed over her. A discreet gesture, but the glint gave him away.

"I've studied the victims, visited their homes and examined their habits and social circles," Bryn began. "All four women had noble goals, lofty ones even. Women of perseverance and dedication to their dreams. Wealthy. Strong. Leaders. I admit, you can't help but admire them."

"I believe women should raise strong women. Nothing would please me more than to see my own daughter mayor one day." The mayor's full lips pulled back, and a mouthful of teeth greeted them as he smiled. His ebony skin matched his suit. "Do you have children, Agent Eastman?"

Bryn shifted and rubbed her hands together. "No."

He turned to Eric. "You, Detective?"

"Not yet. But one day." Eric glanced at Linden again. "What about you? Any daughters?"

"Two."

Bryn continued. "After sifting through their social circles, it came to my attention that you might have had some interaction with these women, if only professionally. Is there anything that might have struck you about them that could be beneficial to us?"

The mayor leaned back on the couch, stroked his chin.

"I knew Kendra on a professional and personal level. She loved her family. Seemed to carry her career and mother-hood in a well-balanced way. She helped with campaign tactics."

"What about Annalise Hemingway? I know she spent her energies on female clients, but would you know anything about her?"

Linden leaned forward. "Why would the mayor know anything about a divorce attorney that set out to devour men? He's married."

Devour men. Interesting terminology. The guy had zero respect for women based on his bawdy reaction to Bryn.

Bryn smirked. "She takes high-profile cases. You know high-profile individuals. Probably golf with some of them. Which reminds me, would either of you know a Julian Proctor?"

"Of course. He's the best cardiothoracic surgeon around. Good man." The mayor gave an affirmative nod.

Bryn glanced at Linden. "And you? Do you know him?"

"I do. He's one of the 'I probably play golf with him' acquaintances." A smug smile spread across his face. Was this guy part of the coalition? Something in his eyes scraped against Eric's nerves.

"Is he a suspect? Because I find that preposterous." The mayor sat his coffee cup on the tray.

"Do you know about his coalition? M.A.G.E., Males Against Gender Equality?"

The mayor grimaced. "I didn't know he had an actual organization, but I'm aware that he doesn't necessarily think women should be involved in politics, the military or high-intensity jobs that males may be more suited for. Differences of opinions, of course. But it's our diversity in this country that makes us great."

"I find unity makes a stronger front line, sir." Bryn's tone oozed like syrup.

He smiled. "Unity on the front line brings freedom. Freedom's fruit is diversity. Individualism. We can all agree to disagree. I disagree wholeheartedly with Julian's ideals on women."

"Did you know Cat Weaver beyond sitting on the same board with her at Rhodes?"

"I've had brief contact with her. Smart woman. Quiet mostly. When she spoke, you'd do well to listen."

Bryn glanced at Eric. So far he was identifying with each woman. Praising them a little more than necessary.

"And obviously you knew Bridgette from the morning show." Bryn pulled out a notepad. "Did you know she was pushing for Tawdle's removal to cast an all-female show?"

"I'm not surprised. Bridgette was cutting-edge. And most viewers are women. Stay-at-home moms," Linden said.

Bryn clenched her jaw. "I guess that brings us back to Annalise Hemingway. You never said how you knew her, if indeed you did. I apologize if we've wasted your precious time. I suppose we could have gathered all this information without your cooperation."

Nice move, Bryn. If the mayor was tempted to lie about his connection to any of these women, Bryn had politely informed him that she'd know. To be caught lying would only make him appear guilty.

The mayor cleared his throat, visibly uncomfortable. He shared a brief exchange with Linden. "Several months ago, my wife and I had some trouble. She threatened divorce. Mind you, she was angry at the time—she'd never go through with it. Anyway, I found a business card for Miss Hemingway in her purse. She'd seen her once. But we reconciled."

"Did your wife see someone new after Miss Hemingway was murdered?" Bryn asked.

Indignation settled concretely in the mayor's eyes. "Like

I said, we reconciled. Agent Eastman, I'm starting to wonder if you want my insight or my alibis for these murders."

Bryn spread a toothy grin. "I'd take both if you're offering."

He stood. "I'm not. Now, if you will see yourself out. I'm a busy man, working for the people of this great city. I do not have time for trifling questions...or for murdering four women." He turned on his heel and strode from the room.

Linden reached the door. "If you want the mayor's whereabouts for the murders, get a warrant." His lips peeled back. "Have fun securing it. The mayor plays cards every other Friday night with the deputy director." He used his hand to dismiss them from the office.

Eric walked Bryn out. She was seething, much like the sky at the moment. "Well...that went well. So much for poking around invisible-like."

"I'd like to add John Linden to our list. He's connected to the same women, if only through Mayor McLoud, and he's an actual friend of Julian Proctor. I wouldn't be surprised if he isn't on the board of that idiotic coalition." She plucked a tube of lip balm from her purse and smeared it on her lips, then hopped on the phone and had Percy dig up everything on John Linden, particularly his connections to the victims, Julian Proctor and Rusty Beckham. She hung up and dug her keys from her purse. "I'm parked over there. I'll meet you back at the field office."

"I thought you had somewhere to be. Isn't that why you drove separate?" Eric tried to keep the hurt from his voice. Looked like Bryn did want distance.

Bryn fidgeted with her key ring. "I needed a breather. You. Me. The time we're spending together. It isn't easy."

Eric nodded and murmured, "I know." He longed for it to be, though. "You want me to walk you to your—"

"I'll be fine."

Eric nodded and glanced up as thunder rumbled. "Storm's coming. Drive carefully." He trudged to his car and climbed inside. Uneasiness spread across his gut. He couldn't be sure if it was this new line Bryn had drawn between them or the tugging feeling that something sinister was in the air besides a storm.

Bryn mentally kicked herself for hurting Eric. He hadn't hid it well. The conversation about his dad and the hate involved... If they ever tried to be more, it would be a slow death. She couldn't handle it. Couldn't handle the nearness and she'd resolved to keep her feelings on a business-only level. The separate cars were a beginning.

The clouds continued to roll in, heavy and gray. Rain pelted her. Shrieking at the chilly drops, she hurried to her car as the bottom opened up on her. She hit the fob, unlocked her door and jumped in, slamming her door shut as pelts turned to sheets. Tossing her purse on the passenger seat with her gun, she clicked her seat belt in place, glanced in the rearview mirror and frowned as her reflection, and not the cars behind her, came into view.

Her breath faltered.

She grabbed for her weapon but couldn't reach it as a garden hose wrapped around her throat like a constricting snake. Gripping the hose, she tried to loosen it, but her attacker continued to squeeze. Bryn's throat ached and burned, her eyes watered. She fumbled to release her seat belt, hoping to lean forward and gain some ground.

"I warned you, Miss High and Mighty. But you didn't listen," the deep voice hissed. Same voice from the park.

Rusty Beckham. Bryn couldn't see his face. Only hers in the mirror, turning crimson.

Needed air.

She clawed against the hose, working for an inch of breathing room. No way to break free from it.

Spots formed in front of her eyes, heat filled her cheeks. *Honk.*

She laid on the horn, and the voice cursed, then let go of the hose long enough to reach forward and grab her hands. She sucked in a lungful of air and scrambled to open the car door.

Had to get out of the car.

Kicking it open, she worked to slither out. The attacker grabbed her wet hair and tried to yank her back inside. She finally slid out of the car, leaving a handful of hair in his grasp. Her scalp stinging, she booked it toward the building.

A dark SUV whizzed into the lot.

Heart hammering, she thrust her arms out in front of her, as if she could stop the vehicle from crushing her.

Brakes squealed, the smell of rubber on wet pavement singed her nose.

Only an inch of space between Bryn and the grill of the vehicle.

Rain cloaked the windshield. The car door opened, and Eric jumped out.

She ran into his arms.

"What happened? I had a feeling. I had it before I ever left the parking lot, but I ignored it." He released her and scanned the lot.

Bryn rubbed her sore neck and pointed. "Rusty Beckham was inside my car."

Eric shot off toward the back of the parking lot. Bryn followed. Rain continued to mercilessly beat on them. Hair matted to her face, clothes clinging, Bryn tailed Eric to her car where Rusty had been.

"I didn't see him. He had my rearview turned, so I couldn't identify him. But I recognized his voice. From the park." It had to be him.

Eric inspected the car. "He's long gone now." Glancing at Bryn he must have just noticed her neck. His eyes widened. Gently, he touched the bruising. Bryn didn't need a mirror to know it was already turning purple. "What did he do to you?" Fury laced his quiet voice.

Bryn shivered. Partly because of the cold. Partly over the fear that still lingered in her veins. Scott Mulhoney's face and the grip around her throat as he woke her from sleep kept her shivering. She told him how Rusty tried to strangle her with a garden hose.

Nostrils flaring, water slicking down his scruffy cheeks, he raked a hand through his drenched coal-black hair. "We're not driving separate anymore. Not ever again."

Bryn simply nodded and fell back into his arms. The downpour might as well be nonexistent. All she felt was the beat of his heart and the safety of his arms. She wouldn't think about how cold and miserable she would feel when he released her.

Or that Rusty Beckham had once again gotten away to plan another attack.

TWELVE

A week had passed. Bryn's sleep had been fitful and she'd taken the sedatives twice, but falling asleep terrified her. She was now seeing Scott Mulhoney's face, along with Rusty Beckham's and Julian Proctor's. Even with Holt in the house most nights, Bryn was on edge. Every threat on her life was one more nail in her coffin.

The crime scene unit had done a thorough search of her car and found particles of soil and chemicals consistent with those used at the garden store and on lawns. It was Rusty. SAC Towerman was allowing her to stay on the case. Regardless of the danger that surrounded her, Bryn had made more links and connections than anyone had before she came on board. The attack on her life cushioned Towerman's reprimand for going after the mayor. After all that, the mayor had the nerve to call and complain. And that kept her from ruling him out.

Fear couldn't paralyze her life or she'd fail. Dr. Warner couldn't keep her from staying in the field. Not if she could keep her sanity and solve this case, confirming the field was where she belonged.

She'd compromised and shared personal information with the doctor, hoping it would benefit her. And now she'd made a compromise with Eric. Bryn would drive herself to and from work, but during the day they would ride together and either Holt would be at the house when she got there or Eric would follow her home and help her clear it. It felt slightly overprotective and yet necessary.

Another case had called Eric away for a few hours, and she'd busied herself going over files and breathing down her analyst's neck, driving him crazy.

This was ridiculous.

She couldn't be escorted around her entire life, and Holt had called earlier. He would be at the house by bedtime. Her stomach cramped anyway. Her home had been invaded before. She grabbed her keys and strode through the parking lot, using extra caution and facing her fears head on.

The only upside was that the sun was shining on this Friday afternoon. Too bad her insides weren't so sunshiny. Wednesday's visit to her alma mater had cast dark clouds over Bryn.

Her life had made a sharp turn since her swim days. Sadly, it was the good times she remembered at Rhodes that had sent her further into a funk. Like the memory of when Holt had come to her first home swim meet and brought Eric. She'd always had a crush on him, flirted heavily, but it was a no-go.

Until she turned nineteen.

They won their meet and a big group had gone out for pizza. Holt and Eric had shown up. Bryn's stomach had erupted in a wild dance and her heart raced faster than when she'd been competing.

Reid Darcy monopolized her time, and Eric had walked right up, showed his badge. *"Excuse me, but I need to ask Miss Eastman a few questions."*

Reid's eyes grew to the size of flying saucers. What would Eric want to ask her about? The first scary thought was Rand had done something. But she never shared that with anyone. Had she gone with her gut, who knew? Abby might be alive.

Eric led her outside the Pizza Hut.

"What's going on, Eric? Or should I say, Detective Hale?" She couldn't help flirting. Bryn was completely taken with his ebony hair and warm brown eyes, not to mention his broad shoulders, muscular arms and chest.

"I was thinking we should ditch the pizza and go for a ride."

"As in downtown?"

Maybe at that moment, when he dazzled her with a grin, Bryn had fallen in love with him. Or at least ruined her heart for any other man.

"As in for ice cream or a movie."

"Are you asking me out on a date, Eric Hale? And pulling the cop card to do it?"

"Gotta do whatever it takes to get to you." He leaned in, the smell of his cologne sending warm fuzzies all over. *"Is it working?"*

It had worked. And at the end of the night, when he'd taken her back to the dorm and kissed her, the world stopped on its axis and she realized she'd never really been kissed before. Boys had kissed her. But there'd been nothing boyish about Eric's kiss. He wasn't hurried. In fact, he'd almost been strategically lazy about it, letting it build and burn until Bryn wasn't sure she'd be able to put the fire out. She hadn't needed to.

Eric, the perfect yet passionate gentleman, had done it for her, gently breaking away, but the burn had continued to blaze in his eyes, the same one that still burned in Bryn's heart.

"Guess you've decided I'm not a little girl anymore."

"You should give me a medal. It's been excruciating waiting for you." After one more lingering kiss, he pecked her nose and told her he'd call. And he had. Every day for the next two years.

Then Abby died.

Bryn couldn't blame walking the halls of her old college on her lingering thoughts of the past. Being back in Memphis and working with Eric had caused them. Dr. Warner had asked her earlier today what she planned to scrape off her full plate.

She had no answers.

She turned into her subdivision after a long, weary day.

They still couldn't get a list of the members belonging to the M.A.G.E. coalition. Rusty Beckham continued to be MIA. The mayor gave them his alibis for Cat Weaver's and Annalise Hemingway's murders. They checked out. Unless he paid Rusty, he wasn't their guy. He'd offered them access to whatever they wanted, including his financials. Brazen thing for a politician to do, but his attorney had advised him to cooperate. Probably to keep them from barking up his tree and stumbling upon secrets he wanted to keep hidden. John Linden, on the other hand, wasn't offering anything, which raised a red flag. Bryn pulled into her driveway. Eventually, she was going to have to clean out that garage if she wanted to park inside it.

She unlocked her door. The day had taken a toll on her, exhaustion setting into her muscles. She froze in the entry.

Newton wasn't barking.

Bryn's heart beat in her temples. "Newton!"

The baby gate was secure, but he wasn't there. She jumped it and searched each room, hollering his name. Her chest clamped like a vise.

Retrace your steps, Bryn. Calm down.

She'd fed him while making coffee. He'd chewed on a shoe, and she put him outside to do his business and wear the friskiness out of him before she left.

Had she brought him back inside? She couldn't remember. Percy had called, then her mother. Surely she had. Newton was her baby. Bryn flew out the back door. "Newt?"

She ran her sight across the fenced-in backyard. Was he scared? Angry? She walked the yard and around to the side.

No! The gate was cracked. She'd been gone since seven this morning. He could be anywhere. Anything could have happened to him.

She tapped her forehead with her fist over and over. How could she be this stupid? This scatterbrained? "Newton!" she hollered and raced next door. Hands trembling, she knocked on their door. No one answered. She checked with her other nearby neighbors. No one had seen her baby.

She jumped in the car and drove around the subdivision calling his name. After circling three times, she pulled over on the side of the road. Tears welled in her eyes. She couldn't even keep a pet. How could she be a good mother? If her womb hadn't been snatched from her. Is that why God let this happen? He knew she'd be a lousy mom? Lose her child. Condemnation's meaty paws pressed on her shoulders, punched at her chest and scratched her mind.

She reached for her phone and called Eric. The only person she wanted.

One ring.

Two.

"What's up? Catch the killer?"

"Help me," she cried.

"I'm on my way. Where are you? Are you hurt? Talk to me Bryn!"

"It's Newton. I—I can't find him. I'm a terrible mother." She couldn't control the sobs. Everything compounding. "I'm in the subdivision."

"Go home. I'll be there in fifteen minutes."

He was at least twenty-five minutes away.

The sound of sirens blared over the phone.

He was pulling out the cop card again.

To get to her.

* * *

Eric's heart rate continued to rise as he whipped into Bryn's subdivision. What was up with the babbling about being a bad mom? The past couple of days her eyes mimicked a raccoon's. She needed more sleep.

If only she'd confide in him. Why wouldn't she trust him with whatever was going on or where she went on Friday mornings that kept them from getting coffee or starting earlier than 10:00 a.m.? How long should he go without intervening? Without poking around in her past or following her?

He wanted answers without having to resort to investigating her like a person of interest. He wanted her to willingly open up. If it progressed, though, he wouldn't have a choice.

Bryn paced the front yard. Eric jumped out, and she lunged into his arms. "Where could he be? I've been hollering until I'm hoarse."

He embraced her, stroked her hair and inhaled her signature orange-and-vanilla scent. "We'll find him. Walk me through your day. Calm down."

Slender yet muscular arms wrapped around his back and showed no intention of releasing, so he held her. This was the way it should've always been. For better or worse. Now being a worse moment. Finally, she broke away. "I must have forgotten to let him back inside this morning, and the gate's open."

"Did you unlock it?"

"No, but Holt and I were hauling stuff out of storage the other night. He probably forgot. Or I did. Probably me."

"I'm sure he's fine."

She pressed her eyes with the heels of her hands. "You don't understand. Newton…he's *all* I have."

So very untrue.

"Have you talked to the neighbors?"

"Yes. Twice. Once while waiting for you. They haven't seen him. He's only a few months old. What if someone stole him? Or ran him over? What if he's in a ditch whimpering with a broken leg?" With each scenario her voice rose.

"Okay, let's not go there just yet. Have you canvassed on foot?"

"No."

"You do that, and I'll do a drive-through." On the main highway. If Newton did get that far and was hurt, the last thing Eric wanted was for Bryn to discover him—and alone.

She nodded and sprinted down the street.

After a thorough search on the main roads, Eric circled back into Bryn's subdivision. "God, please help us find this dog. She's beside herself, and she's hiding something that's getting the best of her. I don't know what it is. But You do." Bryn refused to give him access, and it stung.

He slowed near an abandoned house. A feeling tugged his gut. "Lord, do You want me to stop?" Eric parked the car and slipped through the yard; the sun dipped low on the horizon, and the temperatures had dropped. Puffs of air escaped his lips and floated away on the crisp breeze. Making his way to an old doghouse, he called for Newton.

A scratching noise came from the dilapidated shelter. "Newton, is that you, bud?" Could be a rabid animal. Just what he needed, to end the night with a rabies shot.

A golden head poked out...and barked. "Here, boy!"

Newton scrambled from the doghouse and jumped into Eric's arms, licking his face. "I wonder if I'll get this much enthusiasm from your owner." He scratched the pup's ears as he walked to the Durango. *Thank You, Lord, for helping me find him.* Bryn trudged up the road with slumped shoulders as Eric turned into her drive. He tucked Newton in his arms and stepped out of the Durango.

"Look who I found."

Her head flew up, and she darted into the yard. "Oh! You rotten, lovable, sweet thing."

"You are talking to me, right?"

She beamed, and it connected with his heart. She scooped Newton into her arms and kissed all over him. Didn't look like she was going to pass the love Eric's way.

"Where'd you find him?"

"The doghouse. Literally. Over on Brambleberry."

She continued to plant kisses on her puppy as they went inside. She put him down, and he went straight for a chew toy. She turned and slung her arms around Eric's neck.

Maybe it *was* his turn for kisses, and if she wanted to scratch his head, he wasn't above it.

"I don't know how to thank you."

He had a few good ideas. "You're welcome."

"I owe you two dinners. I know. I'll cook for you." She continued to lock her arms around his neck, but she leaned her head back to peer into his eyes.

"Really?" He turned his nose up. "You want to cook for me? What happened to thanking me?"

"I can cook...now." She shot another glorious smile at him.

He held her tighter, pulled her closer. "And just what can you cook?"

"Spaghetti. Meatloaf—without onions—I know you hate them. Tuna casserole. Homemade macaroni and cheese."

He veered closer to her lips. Couldn't help it. They drew him like honey. He paused before making contact. "Are you happy now, Bryn?"

"Yes," she breathed.

"Then that's all I need." He pressed his lips to hers,

and she bristled, then unlocked her arms and wiggled free from his embrace.

"I'm—I'm sorry."

"No. It's me. I got caught up in a moment. We're—we're working together." Her cheeks had turned crimson, and she raked her hand through her long hair. He'd been an idiot. Should have known better. What if she had felt more for him? What if she had let him kiss her? How was that fair to her? To bring her into a family that hated her.

What would holidays look like?—if they were even invited. Chances were his parents would disown him, and wouldn't that make a great conversation piece with their children. *Why don't we see Grandpa and Grandma? Well, kids, your mom's brother killed your aunt Abby. And they just can't forgive your mom.* The guilt Bryn would feel every day would be unbearable. Eric was being selfish. Trying to fool himself that it might work.

It was just as unfair that they couldn't be together, though. They were adults. But she had rejected his kiss. Bryn may not want to rekindle anything, not because of their past, but because she was over him in that way. The thought sickened him.

"I'm sorry anyway." For so many things.

"Me, too." Did she mean it the way he did? "This isn't going to get awkward, is it? I mean, we're friends, right?"

"Right. It's fine." Only it wasn't. But it'd have to be. Eric stepped back, putting some space between them. "Total slipup."

"We have a history. It's bound to happen, Eric. And…I don't think we'll ever stop being attracted to one another."

Well, at least she thought that much if nothing else. Eric grinned. "Never."

She laughed, and the strain in the room lifted. "Have you had dinner?"

"Actually, I was on my way to eat with friends. My

partner is back in town. The cruise is over, but the honeymoon is not."

"Oh. Have fun, then."

"I was going to invite you anyway. Come with. You'd be doing me a favor. I'm not sure I can handle all the mush, and if it gets to be overbearing, you can fake being sick."

"Why don't you fake being sick?"

"You can only pull that stunt so many times before they catch on."

Bryn snorted and set her attention on Newton.

"Bring him. They won't care." Bringing her to Luke and Piper's would only garner questions from them, but he didn't want to leave Bryn alone. Rusty Beckham was a palpable threat, and until they found him, she wouldn't be safe. And then there was the selfish side of Eric. The side that wanted all the time he could squeeze in. When the case was over, he wouldn't see her every day.

"Are you sure? I mean after..." She pointed from her to him.

"The sorta-might-have-been-a-kiss that shouldn't have happened?" He batted his hand in the air. "Psssht. Water under the bridge."

She twisted her lips to the side and eyed him. "Let me freshen up and change. Ten minutes?"

"Fine."

Pausing at the bedroom door, she faced him—eyes filled with moisture. "You turned your sirens on."

His ribs closed in on his heart. "Gotta do whatever it takes to get to you," he murmured.

Bryn's nerves hummed. Why did this feel so much like meeting parents? Hugging Newton closer to her, she shivered in the cold as Eric rang the doorbell to Luke and Piper Ransom's home.

"I probably should have brought dessert or something."

"You want them to like you, don't you?"

Bryn pelted Eric in the side. "I can make desserts now."

"Can you?" He raised his right eyebrow. Complete skeptic. She most certainly could. A box mix counted, right?

His easy banter relaxed her frayed nerves. "Yeah."

"I'm a Woman" came to mind, and she sang a few lines. She was a working woman and she could bring home the bacon. Frying it up in the pan was the issue.

Eric cackled and jumped in on the chorus. "W-o-m-a-n."

Bryn laughed as they fell into an old but fun habit of singing duets—terribly. She pointed at him and added some attitude in her face, popping her neck to the side, letting him know she could make a man out of him.

"Say it ain't so," he quipped.

That's when the cough broke them out of their duet.

A big guy stood in front of them, about the same height as Eric, only a little gray at his temples and blue eyes that bordered on green. He leaned against the door frame, a curious expression on his face.

"Luke Ransom." He held his hand out for Bryn to shake. "And if you can make a man out of him, I'll give you a million dollars."

Eric slapped his shoulder in a brotherly gesture. "You don't have a million dollars."

Bryn shook his hand, her face flaming. "Bryn Eastman." Newton poked his head from her coat. "This is Newton. Hope it's okay we brought him."

Luke welcomed her into his house. "Of course. I've been wanting a dog." He rubbed Newton's head. "He's cute. Maybe Piper will fall in love and let me get one. Does he chew stuff up?"

Bryn bit her lip. "I'd be lying if I said he didn't."

"It's not looking good for me." Luke grinned.

Bryn put the pup down. "Behave, boy."

"Boys don't behave. Ever." A ridiculously fit woman

breezed into the living room. A fresh sun-kissed glow covered her bare arms and a few blond highlights streaked her brown hair. Honeymoon looked good on her. She gave Bryn's hand a firm shake. "I'm Piper Ransom." She beamed at Luke, her voice a raspy alto. "Never get tired of saying that."

"Good. You've got a lifetime of it."

Eric groaned, one nostril flaring and his upper lip curling. "Bryn, you feeling sick? I thought you said you had a stomachache."

She did actually, but it wasn't from the mush. Okay, it was from the mush. The pangs in her stomach came from knowing she'd never have that with Eric. "I'm fine for now." She turned to Piper. "Bryn Eastman."

"So nice to meet you." Newton jumped on Piper's leg, and she bent to scratch behind the puppy's ears. "Luke wants a dog. I'm not ready for housebreaking it, and I know that'll be my job." She cut her eyes at Luke, and he wiggled his eyebrows.

"It'll be practice for when we have babies."

"Are you saying I'll have to housebreak them, too?"

He kissed her cheek. "I'm saying I want dogs and babies."

Bryn was about to confess a stomachache. Too much baby talk. Eric's eyes had lit up at the mention. "What's for dinner?" he asked, and Bryn wanted to hug him for the subject change.

"I'm cooking my Mama Jean's recipe for chicken potpie and homemade yeast rolls," Piper said.

"That sounds wonderful. Can I help you in the kitchen?" Bryn asked.

"She can fill a mean glass of ice." Eric tugged her hair and winked.

She scowled and followed Piper into the kitchen. "I can do more than fill glasses with ice."

"I take everything Eric says with a grain of salt." Piper opened the freezer door and grinned. "But all that's left to do is fill the glasses with ice."

Bryn helped Piper, then poured sweet tea as they made small talk about Piper's dojo and her program to help at-risk teens. They brought the food and drinks and took their seats around the farm table—one of the only old things in the house.

"So what's it like working with Eric? Does he drive you as crazy as he does me?" Luke asked.

Bryn smirked and buttered a roll. "He drove me crazy long before I worked with him."

Piper laughed and fed Newton a bite of chicken. "That's okay I hope. Guess I should have asked." If Bryn had to guess, Piper and Luke would have a dog before Christmas.

"No that's fine. I spoil him all the time." She relayed the events that led her to bringing Newton, but she passed on the personal moment. The moment when Eric had pressed his lips to hers, like a host of balloons launched. Airy and beautiful.

Piper and Luke tag-teamed as they shared about their cruise, from the sandy beaches to the cuisine and snorkeling. "Took us forever to get to this place, but God brought us together. Again."

Luke cradled her hand and kissed it.

Bryn glanced at Eric. "Again?"

Eric set his tea on the table. "Luke and Piper dated back in the day. Got back together a year ago."

"How'd that happen?" Bryn was a sucker for happy endings.

"Luke suspected me of murder and beating up my grandma." Piper's lips twitched.

"It wasn't *exactly* like that, Bryn," Luke said with a grin on his face. "She exaggerates. About everything. I was working a case that brought us back together. And here we are."

"Sounds like an interesting story."

Piper stood and took her plate and Luke's. "Come help me with the coffee and dessert, and I'll tell you all about it. The whole *un*exaggerated truth."

Bryn took Eric's plate and hers, then followed Piper from the dining room into the kitchen. "So you and Luke dated once before?"

Piper grabbed a container of Cool Whip from the refrigerator. "We were young. I was involved with a bad crowd, and he was working undercover." She removed the plastic and tore the lid off before smothering the cake with it. After finishing the incredible story, she pointed the spatula at Bryn. "What I thought was going to end in a second heartbreak turned out to be a fresh start. We hurdled the obstacles because God gave us the strength to do it. He was faithful, even when we weren't."

Bryn gnawed her lower lip. "What if the obstacles can't be hurdled?"

Piper clasped Bryn's hands. "Every obstacle can be jumped, even if you knock them down or trip. I'm living proof. And Eric, while a goof most of the time, is pretty smart and extremely merciful. I don't see him not wanting to jump a hurdle."

Bryn bit the inside of her lip. "He doesn't know about the biggest one. And I can't tell him."

"Whatever it is," Piper said and squeezed Bryn's hands before releasing them, "he deserves the chance to make the choice. If he loves you, it won't matter."

Bryn groaned. "But it does matter. It will matter. Maybe not at first. But eventually, he'll resent me. I can't have that, Piper. He deserves to get everything he wants. I can't give him that."

"What if all he really wants is you?"

Bryn held back tears. If only that could be true. She folded a dish towel and laid it by the stove. "I'm scared. And I'm angry…at everything that happened and at God for what He took from me."

"I know you're scared. And I *know* scared." She smiled, her eyes warm and sensitive. "I also know what it's like to be ticked at God. Until you can get past that, you won't see things clearly. Not what you want to hear, I'm sure. But it's the truth. I can't let you walk out of here without hearing it." She rinsed the spatula. "God's patient. And He loves you. Even when it feels like He doesn't. When it seems like He doesn't care at all. I can only tell you this because I've experienced it. But He does love you, Bryn." She tossed the Cool Whip container in the trash and put the spatula in the dishwasher. "He's never given up on you. He's not through with you yet, my friend. He's not through yet."

When Piper hugged her, Bryn's eyes burned with tears. A friend. She hadn't known this woman but for a few hours, and it felt as if they'd known each other a lifetime.

"Thank you for talking to me." For not prying or demanding she divulge the entire story. "And for not judging me for being mad at God."

Piper rubbed Bryn's shoulders. "You're welcome. We all have our moments of anger. We just can't stay that way. A good start to healing would be admitting it to Him, and asking for His help in working past it."

"Won't He be mad that I'm mad?"

"I think He can handle it. But let Him help you past it. Bitterness will eat you alive from the inside out."

That's exactly how Bryn felt. Like something was devouring her. Eating away at her insides until she was nothing but a shell. "Thank you. For understanding."

"Whatever and whenever you need me, you call. Besides, we gotta have each other's backs if we're going to put up with those two out there. United front all the way."

Bryn laughed and picked the cake up while Piper carried the coffee to the dining room. "Dessert and coffee," Piper said as she entered. "Chocolate layered cake. Mama Jean's recipe."

"I do love married life," Luke said, taking Piper in his arms and kissing her neck.

"Bryn can't have any. She has a stomachache." Eric gave her "the eye."

Bryn blew him off with her hand. "I'm not leaving until I have a big whoppin' hunk of this cake."

"Fine." He plopped in his chair, feigning indignation. "Cut me a piece, too, then. And don't be stingy about it."

Eric was thankful his friends had made Bryn feel welcome. The moment Piper led her into the kitchen she'd relaxed and stayed that way the remainder of the evening, although something said in that kitchen must have weighed on her mind. She'd been quiet on the ride back to her house.

"That was fun. I liked them."

"They're likable people. As I am." Eric stroked her upper back. "How you feeling?"

"Better."

He half believed her, but once again he wasn't going to pry.

"I think you and Luke make great partners. He can lean toward the overly serious side, while you..." She cocked her head.

Eric cut the ignition in Bryn's driveway. "Luke's a great partner. Mr. Rule Book. The couple of times he bent them, they backfired."

"Do you bend the rules?" Bryn asked.

"Nah, I just like to make him think I will." He chuckled. "Did Piper share their story with you?"

"Yeah. Lot of odds stacked against them."

But they'd prevailed. Could he and Bryn? "Not everyone can make it past obstacles like they did. Of course, I think they tripped over several of them and knocked a load down on the way to the finish line. But…they did finish."

"Yeah, seems they finished well."

"I think if we examined them more closely, we'd find some scars. I know I have scars, Bryn."

Bryn closed her eyes. "Me, too," she whispered as she touched her abdomen. Eric studied her and wondered about the gesture. She reached for the door handle. Eric covered her hand.

"I know we've had a good time tonight. Relaxed. But Rusty Beckham is still out there, and so is Julian Proctor. I want you to be on guard. Don't let tonight fool you into believing the danger has passed." He frowned. "I don't see Holt's car. I thought he was staying tonight."

The police department and the bureau simply didn't have the manpower to keep an unmarked car on her home every night.

"He is. He texted during dinner to say it'd be pretty late."

Eric clenched his jaw. He hated leaving her. "I should stay."

Bryn's smile quivered. "And give my neighbors a new reason to gossip. Get some sleep. I'll be focused and on alert."

Hesitating, he balled a fist. "I worry."

"I know. I won't lie and say I'm not concerned. I'll be okay, though."

Eric would call Holt as soon as he left and see exactly how long he was going to be tied up. "For any reason, without hesitation, call me."

"I will. And I'll even throw you a bone. Come help me clear the house."

"I was already gonna do that."

"Good. Then you go home. No sleeping in the SUV. I need you fresh tomorrow. You promised to help me paint."

"I don't remember that."

"Funny." She unlocked the door, and he slipped inside, clearing each room, checking under beds. No monsters. No Rusty Beckham.

"Lock your doors," he said when he exited the front door. "I'll see you in the morning."

"I'll be fine. I promise."

But he wasn't fine. "'Night."

Eric drove around the neighborhood a few times. Nothing out of the ordinary, but he couldn't keep the invisible creepy crawlers from skittering over his skin. "God, keep her safe. She won't let me."

Begrudgingly, he headed home to his big, cold, empty house.

THIRTEEN

After washing her face and brushing her teeth, Bryn switched off the light and slid under the covers. A faint sliver of moonlight washed through the miniblinds.

Other than a few pops from the house settling, it was quiet. Newton's breaths came rhythmically. He'd had a big day, too. Bryn was as emotionally frazzled as physically. She peeked at her cell phone.

11:43.

Her eyes grew heavier each second. Her leg jerked as she eased into sleep.

Newton's growl jolted Bryn awake, but it was too late.

Beefy gloved hands wrapped around her throat. She opened her eyes, taking in a man wearing a black ski mask, dark jacket and jeans. She clutched his fists, working to pry them away. With the other hand, she aimed for his eye, digging her thumb into the wet socket.

Her attacker hollered and cursed, and loosened his grip on her neck. She sucked air into her burning lungs and brought her legs up, kicking him in the chest and giving herself time to roll to the side of the bed nearest the door.

But her gun was on her night table.

And her phone.

She burst into the kitchen, the thug hot on her heels. After grabbing a kitchen knife from the block, she hurled herself into the garage, slamming her finger on the button to open the garage door, but it wouldn't budge. Darkness overtook her, eyes not yet adjusting. A flicker of moonlight filtered through the garage windows.

She flung herself into the maze of boxes towering in rows and sank down.

Blood whooshed in her ears, leaving her light-headed. With clammy hands, she gripped the knife tighter.

Heavy footsteps thudded on the concrete floor. Paused.

Just like Scott Mulhoney. Looming over her as she slept. Coiling his hands around her throat.

Stomach tightening, sweat rolling down her temples, she clutched the knife.

It was only a matter of seconds before he found her among the rows of boxes. It had to be Rusty Beckham, but with gloved hands she couldn't be sure.

This wasn't Ohio. Bryn wasn't going to shut down.

Fear slicked the back of her throat in acidy waves, but she leveled out her breathing.

God, if You still care at all, help me think straight.

If she rammed a knife into his chest, she'd never get answers. Wouldn't get the mastermind behind this—Julian Proctor. Beside her foot lay a dumbbell and an ankle weight. She silently set down the knife, picked them up and raised herself from the floor, her heart beating against her chest in a staccato rhythm.

All Bryn had going for her was the element of surprise. It was now or never.

She slung the ankle weight across the garage; it clanged against the metal door and fell to the floor. Taking the last shot she had left, Bryn surged forward while the attacker's attention was focused on the noise. Ramming the dumbbell upside his masked head, she toppled him to the ground and struck him once more until he stopped moving.

She yanked off his mask and stared into an unconscious

Rusty Beckham's face. Racing back into the house, she grabbed her gun, cuffs and phone. With the cell to her ear, she straddled Beckham and cuffed him. Eric answered.

"You said call," Bryn said between shallow breaths.

"On my way. You hurt?"

"Me? No. Rusty Beckham can't say the same thing." She hung up, called backup and checked the time on her phone: 3:22 a.m. Hello, Saturday morning.

Rusty came to and struggled with his cuffs, a stream of foul-mouthed words blew from his tongue. Bryn ignored them. This time, she'd fought. She had overcome the panic. And won. Maybe God was with her after all. *God, I'm going to believe that You helped me. That maybe You haven't abandoned me.* She wasn't sure if that was the case or not, but she was alive.

Headlights glared on the sides of the garage windows. Eric was here.

He barreled through the kitchen door into the garage. Bryn stood, her gun pointed on Rusty Beckham. "You want to do the honors of reading him his rights?"

"I ain't sayin' nothing," Rusty hissed, then spit on the concrete.

Thanks for the DNA, idiot.

He shot off a few more expletives.

Eric motioned for Bryn to proceed, and she read him his rights.

Bringing an arm around her shoulders, Eric sighed. "That's twice in one day you've scared me half to death."

"Then you should be all the way dead."

Eric's gaze warmed Bryn, but there was more than relief in his eyes. She wasn't ready to deal with his feelings. Or hers. Eric must have picked up on it. He turned to Rusty, his jaw hardening, nostrils flaring. "So, how's it feel to get beaten up by a girl? A *girl*, dude."

Eric's words would be like pouring salt into a gaping,

bloody wound. Rusty getting bested by a female. Bryn had to hand it to him—Eric knew how to get a dig in and do it calm and collected.

Rusty ranted and cursed. Eric yanked him up by the collar of his coat. "Your mom should be so proud. You really have a way with words." He pointed to the button on the wall. "Hit that, will ya, Bryn?"

"I tried earlier. The garage door wouldn't go up."

A uniformed officer stepped in. "Looks like it's been messed with and recoded."

Bryn glared at Rusty as he smirked. Maybe she should have used the twenty-pound weights instead of the ten. She was just glad he was caught. That she'd been able to take him down. She'd fought and survived with a level head.

Eric was convinced he was having heart palpitations. When he'd looked at his phone and Bryn's number had popped on the screen, he'd lurched from the bed in a state of panic. But she'd used her brain over brawn to take out Rusty Beckham. Eric couldn't have admired her more.

After hauling Rusty to the station and processing him, Eric and Bryn sat inside the interrogation room across from him. "Tell us about Julian Proctor." Eric demanded.

Rusty jutted his chin out and stared straight ahead.

"Fine. Don't. Either way we've got enough on you to send you straight to the chair. Or lethal injection. We're polite Southern gentlemen so we'll offer you a choice. Of course if we're low on the old injection, you'll get the chair regardless."

Rusty's cheek twitched. Eric was getting through.

"Care to reconsider the silent treatment?"

"What do you wanna know?" Rusty grunted and pursed his lips.

"Why did he bail you out of jail?"

"He's a nice guy." Rusty crossed his arms over his chest and set his jaw.

Eric remained calm. Coming across the table only worked in the movies and in really bad crime novels. Slow and steady would win out. And while he waited, he'd envision coming across the table and wringing this joker's neck.

"Look, you cooperate with us and we'll see if the DA will offer leniency. Maybe take the death penalty off the table. Did he require you to do this as a favor for bailing you out of jail?" Eric faked boredom and cupped his hands behind his neck as if about to snooze in the chair. "I've got all day."

"I ain't gonna get the death penalty for threatening some broad who thinks she's high and mighty."

"Try attempted murder, not threatening," Bryn said and stood, arms akimbo. "And you absolutely will get it for the murders of Cat Weaver, Kendra Kennick, Annalise Hemingway and Bridgette Danforth. So if Julian Proctor put you up to it or is in on it with you, you'd be smart to talk to us. Although, you've proven your lack of intelligence so far."

Rusty's face twisted. "What? You think I did those broads?"

"Give me a reason to think you didn't," Bryn challenged. "You were there the night we found Bridgette Danforth. You attacked me in the park. I drew your tattoo, and you were identified. You shot at me, tried to strangle me, twice…knocked me out and tossed me in a woodpile—"

"You can't prove it!"

Technically, all she could prove was the attack in the park, thanks to the tattoo. She didn't actually see Rusty hit her on the head at the garden store. Recognizing his voice wasn't enough to convict.

"Who will a jury believe? You, a filthy pig, or an up-standing citizen and officer of the law?" Bryn placed her hands on the table and leaned into Rusty's ugly mug. "You're going away, Rusty. It's just a matter of how long and if you spill on Julian Proctor."

He licked his lips and cursed. "I want a lawyer."

And end of interrogation. He probably thought Proctor would hire a fancy attorney to get them out of this. He would probably be right.

"Fine, don't talk. We don't need you to." Bryn blew from the room. Looked like she was planning on waking up a judge for a warrant into Proctor's financials. They'd looked into Rusty's phone records. No calls made to Proctor. Of course, they could have used untraceable burner phones.

No heavy deposits landed in Rusty's account, but he might not have put payouts in an account. Proctor's financials would show him withdrawing large amounts of money if he'd been paying Rusty. If they could find that, they could get a warrant to search Proctor's home, but he was calculating and clever. Using his own home to drown the victims would be stupid. But he might keep his souvenirs there—the jewelry he took from each victim. They hadn't found any at Rusty Beckham's.

Bryn entered the room with a smug smile on her face. Guess she'd gotten her warrant.

Time to cover all the bases. Yeah, he'd asked for a lawyer, but maybe... Eric slid a photo toward Rusty. John Linden left a tart taste in Eric's mouth. On the off chance Julian Proctor wasn't calling the shots, Linden had connections to each victim and had refused access into his financial affairs. Not good.

"Have you ever seen this man?"

Rusty studied the photo. "What if I said I had?"

"Have you?"

"Yeah, I seen him. Who is he?"

"Where have you seen him?" He needed to connect him to a coalition meeting.

"Standing in the back once at a M.A.G.E. meeting. Is that a crime?"

Eric shifted toward Bryn, and motioned for her to follow him outside the room.

"What are you thinking? John Linden is involved?" Bryn asked.

"They wouldn't run from him. Rusty has identified and connected him to the coalition. Plus, he's a hater."

"So is Julian." There were entirely too many haters.

"I know. It's a long shot. Maybe if we get the focus off his mentor, he'll talk before the lawyer gets here."

"And everything he says will be inadmissible and could ruin our case, Eric."

"We were already barking up Linden's tree. I just wanted identification. I got it." He groaned. "I don't want to miss anything. We need to cover all angles. Maybe they're all involved indirectly." Or they all had a part to play with each woman. He shrugged off the ludicrous thought.

"We need that members list. See if Linden is indeed on it."

"Did you see Beckham's face when you pinned those murders on him? He won't deny hating our victims—simply based on gender—but he was shocked. Maybe he came out to see what the fuss was about. Heard it on a scanner or something and then saw you come in and take charge—"

"I did not take charge!"

Eric didn't mean to ruffle her feathers. He clasped her shoulder. "To him you did. So he loses it. Makes it his mission to scare you, but it escalates with each threat. He gets a taste of taking a life and continues to try. He idolizes Proctor, but that doesn't mean he's working with him." Didn't mean he wasn't. Eric wasn't sure who was doing what, but they were all guilty of something.

"Two killers or three, but not working together. You think the threat on me is over?"

"It wasn't Rusty who locked us in the steam room. You're getting close to a killer. And the closer you come, the worse it's going to get. Not trying to scare you—"

"Too late. Hey, I don't have a death wish. Fear can be a motivator to stay alive."

Good. At least she was being rational about that.

"I won't let anything happen to you. But the minute Proctor realizes we've got Rusty in custody and are focusing on him, he'll take drastic measures. And he's not a loose cannon like Beckham."

"I guess we better catch him quick then."

Easier said than done.

After interrogating and booking Rusty, Bryn and Eric had spent the rest of the day combing through Julian Proctor's phone records and financials. The man was squeaky clean and that didn't jive with Bryn. A guy like that was bound to have some skeletons in his creepy woman-hating closet.

Sunday, she spent most of the day sleeping off the exhaustion. Eric had invited her to church, but she declined and then felt guilty for it. The rest of the week had been a blur and they were no closer than they were last Saturday. Actually, they were more confused.

They'd received a warrant for the members list, and John Linden was on it. The judge had given them a long leash and a warrant into Linden's financial records, with a strong warning to be discreet. What they found were several large chunks of money withdrawn each month from one of his private accounts. Where was this money going? Nothing had been deposited into Rusty's account or Proctor's. But then maybe they didn't dump it in their accounts. Bryn had Percy working on offshore accounts but so far nada.

Today, she sat in the club chair in Dr. Warner's office staring at the fish and giving him the rundown of last week-end's events, including her ability to think straight and get the upper hand on Rusty Beckham. That should prove she could perform in the field permanently.

Dr. Warner had taken his usual position on the couch. One leg cocked over the other.

"I believe we're closing in, but he—they—whatever. They're smart. I hate when killers are smart."

"I suppose that's why they get away with it the longest." Bryn grunted.

"Are you frustrated? You want to talk about it?"

If it would convince him that she had it together, then yes. "When I heard Newton growl, I couldn't wake fast enough. But I didn't have time to think about Scott Mulhoney. I had to fight. Once I got to the garage, though, I had time to feel the fear sink in and paralyze me. I wasn't sure I could do it. I hadn't done it before. And then I knew. I'm not a victim. I'm a survivor. I'm stronger."

Dr. Warner jotted a note and leaned forward. "Stronger than…?"

"Than I was then. Each attack is meant to make me weak and afraid, but he's doing the opposite. He's only fueling my fire."

Dr. Warner studied her. "And your forgetfulness and slips of conversation? Gaining clarity or not?"

Dr. Warner's point landed straight in the heart like a stake to a vampire. Even after proving she could fight and win, she'd still been misplacing things. Little things. But they were adding up and piling on top of all her other stresses, freaking her out.

Sweat popped along her hairline, and a cold chill swept over her clammy skin. Was she riding a false sense of security? What if the stress snapped her in two and she broke down completely?

"Agent Eastman?"

She bent forward and breathed deep, unable to pull it

together, to control the rapid heart rate or the sensation of heavy sandbags on her chest. Dr. Warner couldn't see this. But the anxiety didn't care and raged on. "I'm fine."

"You're having a panic attack. You're not fine. Breathe in. Breathe out." He walked her through it and sat back, her file next to him.

She looked him in the eye and knew. It was over. And could she blame him for making this call? Bryn had come in strong and sure and instead of giving him proof, she'd been overwhelmed and let her insecurity show him panic. If one of those hit her in a critical situation, she could end up dead. Civilians could. Eric, even. But she wasn't ready to throw in the towel. "I know what you're going to say. You'd be wrong, Dr. Warner."

"I'm going to recommend you return to office duty only. Until you can declutter your head. We'll continue our sessions."

Bryn jumped up. "No. One panic attack isn't enough to shove me in the office."

"Has it only been one?" He calmly held her stare.

There'd been a few. She kept silent, refusing to lie, but confessing seemed like betraying herself.

Dr. Warner folded his hands in his lap. "You're suffering from mild cognitive impairment, and it's interfering with your ability to do daily tasks. It's worsened as the stakes have risen. The more complicated and demanding the job is, the worse it'll become. Your panic attacks will increase. I'm going to prescribe you Xanax."

"But it's not interfering," Bryn protested. "Look how far I've gotten on this case."

"Bryn, you left your dog outside, and it wandered off. The one thing you consider most valuable, you neglected."

Bryn swallowed the burning lump in her throat. He was right. Rubbing her temples, she leaned back in the chair.

There had to be something she could do to convince him. To prove otherwise.

"I have a meeting scheduled with SAC Towerman to discuss your progress on Monday." Dr. Warner leaned forward. "If after a year you progress, we can go from there." He checked his watch. "Time's up."

Ain't that the truth.

She wasn't going down without a fight. She balled her fists. "So maybe I have mild cognitive impairment. You can fix it."

"You need less stress. This case is more than you can handle."

"You think he's going to stop coming after me because I'm behind a desk? I've blazed a trail right toward him. He won't forgive that. Either way, the stress is there. I've gotten further than anyone. I have a profile—wealthy, Caucasian male age thirty to forty-five."

"Agent Eastman—"

She had to fight! "I know he's prominent in the community. He's able to blend in with the elite without creating fear. He hates women. Probably had a mother abused by a tyrannical husband who instilled his beliefs in his son. I think those beliefs were backed up by a series of rejections from women both professionally and personally. And that was all before I came across Julian Proctor."

Dr. Warner closed his notebook with finality and stood.

Bryn's insides burned. Yes, she'd been forgetting things and slipping up but she was focused—enough to bring closure. "I'm not a quitter."

"You're not quitting, Agent Eastman. You're taking time to restore your mental health."

"If you take me off this case, women will continue to die. He's stopped following his bimonthly pattern. Time is of the essence. The fact I'm a woman closing in on this animal has got to stick in his craw. He'll slip up when it hits

him a woman is beating him at his own game. A woman!"
She took a deep breath, gained some composure. "Let me
find this pathetic excuse for a man and bring justice to
those women. They deserve it. Their families deserve it."

Dr. Warner formed a steeple with his fingers and placed
them on his lips. Had she changed his mind? Could he see
her passion and conviction? She could see the wheels turning in his eyes.

"I'm not your enemy, Agent Eastman. But I can't skew
the evaluation because of your passion."

Bryn's world tipped. Not her enemy? Maybe not. But
he was the concrete wall she'd slammed against. The grief
traveled from head to toe.

"I expect to see you twice a week now, for good measure. We'll reevaluate in six months if the panic attacks
cease and then in another six."

Gaping, she shook her head. His words like fuzz in her
brain. *Six months? A year?* Everything she'd worked for—
robbed. Bryn had been managing. Fighting. For her. For
these women. Clamping the inside of her bottom lip with
her teeth to keep it from quivering, she gave him a single
nod. She'd truly believed he'd been an obstacle she could
get around.

But she hadn't.

She walked out of the office in a zombie-like state until
she hit the sidewalk and snapped to attention, not feeling
safe anymore since the shooting.

Behind a desk.

What would she tell Eric? A wave of humiliation washed
heat into her face. Everything she'd tried to keep secret
would now be out. Agents would question why she was
off the case, why someone else was stepping up. They'd
call her weak.

Tears slipped down her cheeks, then turned to sobs.

She had nothing left.

Not even her dignity.

Holt was parked in her drive when she got home. He met her at the door. "You trying to burn the house down?"

"Nooooo." She didn't mask her confusion as she pushed past him and rubbed Newton. "Hey, boy."

"Then don't leave candles burning. If you want to do the girlie thing and soak in the bathtub, fine, but blow the flowery-smelling things out when you're done. You could've sent this place up in flames."

"They were *all* burning?" She thought she'd blown them out after draining the water. Baths with candles always relaxed her, and she'd been wound tighter than she'd ever been.

"No. Just the one."

Chucking her purse on the table, she didn't know whether to crumple on the floor or concede that Dr. Warner might know what was best for her. He wasn't wrong. But he wasn't right, either, if that made any sense.

"What's with you?" Holt hopped onto the counter in the kitchen, nursing a bottle of water. "You haven't been yourself since you got back, and you've been even shiftier since Hale came into the picture. Doesn't take a genius to see you're still into him. What's the problem?"

Bryn frowned. "The problem? Other than his parents hate me and our family history, and not necessarily in that order." Not to mention her career was basically over.

"Big deal. If he's into you—and he is—should it matter? If he's willing to deal with being shunned, why shouldn't you be?" Holt slid off the counter. "Life's short, Bryn. Especially when you love someone. Don't waste the time."

Bryn's heart thumped out of rhythm. Holt ought to know. He spoke from experience. "I'm being insensitive. I'm sorry."

Holt sniffed and shrugged. "Don't be sorry. Don't be stupid, either. Tell him what happened. Because he deserves to know. As a man, and as your partner. Partners shouldn't keep stuff from each other."

They weren't partners. Especially not now. What was she going to tell him? How was she going to tell him? "It's complicated."

"What relationship isn't?"

He had a point.

"I wasn't just shot, Holt. I…I can't have children because of it."

"Bryn." Holt grabbed and hugged her. "I didn't know. I'm so sorry. So very, very sorry."

She cried into his chest, let all the emotion out. Needed to. "Eric wants babies. Loads of them."

"If he loves you, it won't matter. I've known him forever. It won't matter." He stroked her hair. The most tender she'd seen him in a long time.

"Maybe not now but in a year. Five. Ten. He might regret loving me. Marrying me. I couldn't live with that. I won't. And don't you tell him."

Holt released her and wiped a few tears from her cheeks. "I wouldn't do that, and you know it. But what happened doesn't define you. You're still breathing. That…piece of trash didn't take your last breath. You still have life to live. And you should live it with the one you love for as long as you do breathe." Holt swallowed.

"You miss her."

Holt handed her a napkin. "Blow your nose."

She'd crossed a line bringing up his past. Bryn blew her nose and wadded the napkin. "Holt, you're still breathing, too."

Holt's jaw pulsed. "I broke up the tile in the guest bathroom and cleaned it up. I'll be back at some point to lay the new stuff."

Looked as though he wasn't planning on taking his own advice any time soon. "Okay. Thanks."

"You got it, cuz. Blow more than your nose, i.e., candles out after soaking."

"I will."

Holt let himself out. Bryn poured a glass of lemonade and stared at the backyard. Eric did deserve to know what happened in Ohio and why she was having some slipups. He was going to find out anyway when he heard she was off the case. But it was long past time. Fingers trembling, she picked up her phone and called him.

"Hey, you catch the killer?"

If only. It might have kept her in the field. "No. But I need to talk to you. Can you swing by?"

"Sure, but it'll be a couple hours. I'm on my way to the unwed mothers' home. The lady that runs it said Angela left. Got into a green Lexus."

"Baby daddy."

"Yeah, I'm trying to locate her now."

"I'll put on coffee."

"Nice and strong."

"Of course."

"And you could always fry up the bacon…for sandwiches."

"I'll think about it." She hung up. Hopefully, Angela hadn't done anything stupid. And the baby was safe.

At least Bryn had time to try to muster courage. She couldn't blame Eric if her situation changed things for him, but coming off the blow she'd been dealt by Dr. Warner, she wasn't sure she'd be able to handle the rejection.

She was one thread away from snapping in two.

FOURTEEN

Clouds loomed overhead mimicking Eric's insides. Overcast. Chilly. One of these days Angela would listen to him, and Bryn would confide in him. He'd been praying that God would soften Bryn and watch over Angela.

Eric pulled up to the two-story home set in a quiet residential neighborhood. Miriam Haviland met him at the front door. Worry swam in her gray eyes. "I told her to think things through. To call you first." She chewed her thumb. "I've been praying nonstop."

Raking a hand through his hair, Eric sighed. "Tell me what happened. Exactly."

Miriam shook her head, her short blond hair swished against her chin. "She's been stir-crazy since she got here. Kept to herself. But that's normal. She said she wanted some air, and it's not like we hold the women prisoners."

Eric patiently waited as Miriam dabbed her eyes. "I loved her before I ever saw her."

"I know." Eric understood that kind of gift. Same love God knit into his soul every time he worked a Royal Family Kids' Camp. Loved each one as if they were his own. Would take them home with him if he could, and that's what made it so hard to say goodbye after the camp was over. The passion for their safety and love never faded and kept him praying.

"Tamika had been on the porch. Said she saw Angela hurry down that way." She pointed to the west end of the street. "She got into a green Lexus."

"Did Tamika get a good look at the guy?"

"Yes. He was blond. Clean-cut. Angela hopped in, and they disappeared around the corner."

"I need to talk to Tamika."

A woman with smooth mocha skin and a protruding belly came onto the porch. She glanced at Miriam.

"Tell him what you told me," Miriam said.

Tamika shrugged. "Me and Angela share a room. Hit it off pretty good. She told me about the daddy. Rich guy. Said that he been texting her, and told her it was okay if she wanted to have the baby. That he'd take care of them both. But he wanted to see her. To talk about it."

What would change his mind? Nothing. Had to be a ruse. Eric's stomach knotted. Angela could be in all kinds of danger. "Did she give you a name?"

Tamika shook her head. "No. She said it was going to have to stay a secret until the baby was born, so he could plan for them. But she was stoked about it."

"By any chance did you see his tags? Get even a letter or number?" With no name or nothing else to go on, his hands were tied.

"I didn't. I saw his face real clear, though."

"Good. I'm going to get the local police to send a sketch artist." He made a phone call and hung up. "They're sending a guy over now. She never said where she was going?"

"No. But she said that sometimes they met up at a hotel on Elvis Presley. Sometimes he got it for two days and let her crash. He was good to her, mostly. Gave her a monthly allowance. Fifteen hundred bucks."

Probably hush money. If he was as important as Angela said, then he'd have to ensure she kept their relationship—if it could even be called that—quiet. "Did she say how she met him?"

"She was working outside the Peabody hotel, and he was having drinks with colleagues. That's what she called them."

Eric entered a Google search on his phone for hotels and motels on Elvis Presley. He automatically excluded the ones at Graceland. A patrol car edged near the mailbox and a uniformed officer stepped out. An artsy-looking guy with a sketch pad followed.

Tamika sat on the porch swing as the man drew.

"Straight nose. Like him." She pointed to Eric. "Soft lookin' skin like his too. But tanner."

The artist sketched away. "Eyes? Close together, set apart?"

"Blue. Normal?"

"Hair?"

"Short but not buzzed. Kinda slicked back all perfect-like."

Eric snorted. "Sounds like a politician… How much money did you say Angela was receiving a month?"

"Fifteen hundred."

A sick sensation pooled in his gut as he scrolled through his phone. "Is this him?"

Tamika pointed. "Yes! That's the man. That's her sugar daddy."

That was John Linden.

Angela's life might be at stake. Surely Linden wasn't so stupid as to commit murder. But he had zero respect for women. Or life. He probably saw Angela as nothing more than a broken toy he could discard whenever he saw fit.

Where would he have taken her?

Eric wasn't so sure any talking was going to get done wherever it was. Desperate men did desperate things.

God, please keep Angela and her baby safe.

He called Bryn and filled her in. "May be longer than I thought." He'd have to comb one hotel after another near Elvis Presley.

"That's fine. Do you need me to do anything? Call in a favor? Get some extra men on the hunt?" Concern lined her voice.

"You can pray, Bryn. Pray she makes it out of this alive. Her and the baby."

Silence filled the line. "Okay." Her voice sounded weak. Unsure.

"I'll be there as soon as I can."

Frayser. Angela said she was visiting a friend out there the day they met her at Sonic. Why way out there? What if she'd been meeting Linden? Who in Frayser would recognize him? And she had been staying at a hotel nearby. The kind of motel that allowed working girls.

Once again Eric picked up the phone, dread forming a pit in his gut. He was too far out and time was slipping away. He called a favor in from an officer buddy in that area. He'd make it there long before Eric could.

He jumped in his Durango and hit the interstate.

Bryn had drained one pot of coffee and put on another. She'd tried phoning Eric to check on the latest information concerning Angela, but it had gone to voice mail.

Pray.

God's ways made no sense to Bryn. Not that she bore ill will toward Angela, but the woman was unfit to be a mother—at least at this point. Already, damage could have been done to the baby. And yet Bryn was healthy, took care of herself, would never use drugs. She had a good job, decent salary.

If she stayed on the subject too long, she'd go crazy. There was no way to understand God's plans. Simple as that.

Something Piper said sprang to mind.

"I had to realize that God was in control. Even when it felt like He wasn't. Even when I thought I knew better for my life. Even when I was so mad at Him I could scream. I didn't think I deserved the life dealt to me. But without that life, I'd have never met Luke. Never have been in that pool hall. Never would have turned to karate, and I would never have discovered my life's passion—to help neglected and at-risk teens. I'm thankful for my rough past. I can embrace it. Now."

Bryn wasn't ready to embrace the fact she couldn't have children. But her passion had been born from tragedy. Not that God had made a tragedy occur—Rand had—but something good had come from it.

Evil had taken Abby and those two other girls.

So why was she blaming God for taking a piece of her? Because He'd allowed it.

Looking back, swimming had been a love but not a passion. She hadn't realized that until she changed careers. Bringing justice for victims was both. It drove her to wake up every morning, and she was better at it than swimming. Even Eric had chosen to work in homicide and was great at his job.

Some good had come from Abby's death. Could she trust God to bring something good from the shooting? She supposed it boiled down to trust. In the good times but also in the uncertain and bad times. When things were smooth, it had been easy to go to church and trust God with her future. But when tragedy hit, she ran. Fast and far.

Her doorbell rang.

Bryn shook her clammy hands and opened it to Eric. His scruff appeared thicker and matched the color under his eyes. He seemed to need a hug as much as she did. Her stomach twisted. "Angela?"

"She's okay."

"Come in," Bryn murmured. Newton clawed at Eric's

jeans. He snatched him up and grinned. "I see why you like this pup. Not sure I've smiled in the last two hours."

Neither had she. "I made coffee. Again. Have a seat. Did you find her? Was it really John Linden?" Prolong the dreaded conversation.

"Yes to both. The money we thought he might be paying Rusty Beckham was actually cash he paid Angela."

"Unbelievable and yet believable." Bryn brought the mugs to the table. "Hush money, I guess."

"Yeah. But she thought he was taking care of her, that he loved her. The girl has no idea what a real man loving a woman looks like." Eric sipped his coffee. "After he tried to smother her with a pillow, I think she has come to the conclusion that he was lying about everything."

Bryn laid her hand over his. "And now?"

"Couple Frayser police buddies busted in while he was trying to kill her. They found a syringe of heroin. Guess he was gonna stage an overdose. No one would question it."

"The ME would have discovered the drugs had entered her system postmortem."

Eric grinned. "You have a great mind. Linden does not. Or he was going to smother her until she passed out, then administer the lethal dose. Who knows?"

Bryn shook her head. "What's next for Angela? And the baby?"

Eric ran his finger across the lip of his mug. "She's agreed to go to Christian counseling and stay at the unwed mothers' home. Sometimes it takes a near-death experience to scare you straight."

"That brings me to why I want to talk to you."

"You planning on having another near-death experience?" He sobered. "Or have you?"

Her throat convulsed. He deserved the truth. Then after she told him she'd been yanked off the case he could decide…make a clean break.

She swallowed the tightness. "I worked a case in Cleveland. Scott Mulhoney had been stalking women before entering their home, assaulting them and shooting them."

Eric slid his coffee to the side, leaned in and focused on her eyes. The warmth gave her some strength to continue. Or maybe it was God. Or both.

"My job was to go in and help local authorities. I did that. Discovered his identity. Assisted. But Scott Mulhoney slipped through their fingers before they made an arrest, and…"

Eric fisted his hand, his jaw thumped. "And?"

Bryn forced back threatening tears. Could she do this?

Eric squeezed his eyes shut then opened them. "Did he hurt you, Bryn?"

She knew what he was asking. Had she been sexually assaulted? "No." But she had been hurt. "I'd fallen asleep on my couch. He jimmied the window lock and cut through my screen."

Eric reached across the table and gripped her hand.

"It wasn't pretty. I panicked. But somehow I made it to the bedroom. To my gun. He fired first." She touched her abdomen. "I survived his slug. He didn't survive mine."

Eric pushed back his chair, pulled her out of her seat and into the safety of his arms. "I am so sorry." He stroked her hair and kissed the top of her head. "That's why you came back."

"I didn't want to. This job isn't easy for a woman, and I was afraid everyone would think I was weak and unfit to do my duty. Maybe it was my perception, maybe not. Probably somewhere in between, but I had to get out of that house. Out of that state. Holt's here. Some familiarity."

Now many of her colleagues here would think the same things about her she didn't want those in Ohio thinking.

"I understand and I want you to know that I don't think you're incapable of doing your job. Not even when I tailed you home or asked Holt to stay. It had nothing to do with incompetence on your part." He framed her face and forced her to look at him. "You understand that, right?"

Bryn inhaled his scent, saw truth in his eyes. He did care. Which made things so much harder on her. She nodded. "I'm seeing the FBI therapist. That's why I was downtown." She broke away from his touch and paced the breakfast area floor.

"You didn't want me to know because you were afraid I'd think you were falling off the deep end. Incapable of doing the job."

Of course he'd understand. She nodded again. "I have been spiraling off the deep end. Little things. Zoning out. Today? I could have burned down the house. And Newton? I get sick every time I think about that." She paused, her back to him. "I was yanked off the case today. Too much stress, especially with these attacks. I'm going behind a desk for at least six months. And I have to see the therapist twice a week now." She cringed, a garbled cry slipped from her lungs. "They'll be sending you a new agent to assist."

Bryn was done. Washed up.

Eric turned her toward him, steel in his eyes. "You're not spiraling out of control. You're good at what you do. They've made a mistake. I can attest. Write a letter or something."

She touched his face. "It won't matter. But thank you."

"You are amazing, Bryn. You were born to be a field agent. I believe it."

Tragedy had given birth to her purpose. No denying that. "Does Holt know?"

"Everything but the therapy appointments and that I'm off the case."

Eric laced his hands through hers. "I wish I could have been there for you in Ohio. When it happened. Wish I could have been there to stop it."

So did she.

"But you made it out alive, and that's what's important. God saved you, Bryn. Protected you."

Bryn never should have made it to the bedroom. But she had.

"Bryn, there's got to be something we can do to keep you with me." Pain creased his brow. Did he mean on this case or personally? "We're further than we've ever been. I'm honestly grateful for your help. Okay, you zoned out a few times. I filled you in. We make a good team." The longing in his eyes might as well be a lighthouse drawing her to the shore.

"We do," she whispered.

He ran his thumb across her lower lip. "We could stay that way. A team."

She owed him the rest of the story. Instead, she closed her eyes as his mouth met hers.

This wasn't fair to him. To kiss him knowing he didn't have all the facts.

The warmth of his lips sizzled all the way to her toes. Same slow, lingering kiss, but different, too. Stronger. As if kissing a passionate promise into her.

One she couldn't accept until he knew everything.

She pulled away breathless and fearful he would never again look at her as he did this very moment.

She was selfish.

"I shouldn't—"

Pressing a finger to her lips, Eric shook his head. "Don't you dare tell me that was a mistake. It wasn't. Don't let how my parents feel interfere with how you do. I've let it affect me. But I can't. Not anymore."

Bryn closed her eyes. "You need to know something first." She had to tell him. Afraid or not. *God, I'm going to trust you. Please make this end well.*

Eric's phone rang. Once. Twice. He glanced down and

frowned. "It can wait." He shoved his phone in his pocket, but it rang again.

"You need to get that." Bryn rubbed her hands on the sides of her jeans.

"No. Tell me what I need to know. It's Dad. He probably wants to talk golf or ride my case about something."

It rang again.

Eric grabbed his phone and growled. "Hold that thought, Bryn. We're not done yet." He answered. "Dad. This better be good." His face turned ashen. "When? Where are you? Which hospital? I'm on my way."

"What's happened?"

"It's my mom." Eric stared, but Bryn wasn't sure he actually saw her face. Or anything. "She had a heart attack."

"Go! Go. I'll pray." She would.

"Come with me." The desperation in his voice crumbled her, but she hesitated anyway.

"Eric. You and I both know the last thing your family needs is me up in the middle of another tragedy. Go. You're wasting time."

Pain etched across his face. He grabbed her shoulders. "I need you. I want you to be there. You don't have to go in the room. Just knowing you're by my side…"

His words slipped into her soul, warming her. How could she deny him? "Okay," she whispered. "I'll go."

Knots formed in her stomach, and her hands turned clammy. Brooks Hale wouldn't like this at all.

But Eric needed her.

No one was there for her when she was lying helpless on her bedroom floor not knowing if she'd live or die before the ambulance came. She'd been alone in the hospital bed until her parents arrived.

She would be there for him. No one should have to experience fear alone.

FIFTEEN

Eric's mind swirled with hundreds of thoughts. He'd barely had time to process what Bryn had finally been willing to confide, and she hadn't even had the chance to finish the conversation. What if she crawled back in her shell and refused to talk again?

But she was here. With him. This brave, wonderful woman putting aside her feelings for his. Knowing she'd probably have to endure glares as well as thorny words from his father.

He laced his fingers with hers as they raced down the halls of the hospital to the cardiology wing. Antiseptic assaulted his nostrils. Nurses in scrubs buzzed in and out of rooms.

Dad met them in the waiting area. Cheeks sunken, red-rimmed eyes, he appeared every bit his sixty-three years. Eric tightened his grip on Bryn's hand. Dad eyed Bryn, then their hands, but said nothing.

"What happened?" Eric asked.

"We were having dinner at home. I grilled steaks and asparagus. Her favorite." His voice trembled, and Eric realized how much his father loved his mother. He hadn't grown up in an overly affectionate home. Dad had his agenda. Mom had hers. "Head over heels" wouldn't describe them. Even after Abby died, he'd rarely seen Dad embrace Mom.

At least not in public.

"We were discussing a cruise and the next thing I know, she's…" He faced the fluorescent lighting and pursed his lips. "I called an ambulance. Doctor said one of her coronary arteries is completely blocked. They're performing an angioplasty now. But…there's damage. So I don't know."

Eric's own heart missed a few beats. Mom might not make it? Then it struck him. "Who's performing the surgery?" His stomach jumped into his throat. Bryn's eyes widened.

Was it the number one cardiothoracic surgeon in the United States? The woman hater? What if he knew it was Eric's mom and let her die on the table as retaliation? He had told them to tread lightly. A sour taste coated his throat.

Dad sniffed. "Julian Proctor."

God, please don't allow him to let her die. Please, God!

Bryn touched his biceps and whispered, "It's gonna be okay." She looked at Dad. "It's going to be a long wait. I'll get coffee. How do you take it, Mr. Hale?"

He blinked as if he couldn't remember. "I, uh…black."

"I'll be back."

"That didn't look like just working with her." Dad slid into a chair in the corner.

Eric collapsed next to him. "No. It wasn't." Now wasn't the time to discuss it. He pulled a Twizzler from his jacket pocket. "Want one?"

A weak chuckle escaped Dad's lips. "No. When your mom couldn't catch her breath and fell to the floor…I thought I was losing her right before my eyes. I could do nothing."

Eric's eyes burned as his insides continued to twist. Somewhere back there Julian Proctor had Mom's chest cracked open.

Dad hung his head between his knees as if he couldn't catch *his* breath. "All I could think on the way here was

I've been fortunate to love her for all these years. No one else on the earth would put up with me. My hours at the club. But she never complained. Not once." He dragged his hands through his silver hair. "Don't know where I'd be if she'd went with what's-his-name."

Eric turned. "What?"

"She loved someone else when she caught my eye. But I was determined to change that. I'd be lost without her. I feel lost right now."

This was the most emotion Eric had ever seen from Dad. He'd said more in the past five minutes than he had in months. Maybe years. At least words that mattered.

"It was amazing to have Abby as long as I did." He cleared his throat. "Do you love her?"

"Bryn?"

Dad nodded once.

"I'd be lost without her." He prayed they wouldn't lose Mom because of Eric's investigation. Surely, Proctor wouldn't…couldn't…

Dad inhaled and pawed his face. "Then I'm not gonna stop you. Life's too short to not go after your dreams."

Who was this man? Eric gaped. "You've forgiven her?"

"I've come to terms with the fact that she didn't kill my baby girl."

It was more than Eric expected, although he wasn't exactly opening his arms for Bryn. "And Mom?"

"I might have exaggerated her feelings. We'll figure it out as we go. It's hard to see Miss Eastman and not think of what her brother did. But I won't put up a fight or say anything unsavory. It'll take time."

Did Dad have a heart attack, too? Lack of oxygen to the brain? "Thank you." He'd take it. Maybe this was a start to something real.

Bryn tiptoed into the room with two coffees. She handed one to Eric, another to Dad.

Dad accepted it and nodded.

Baby steps. They were in the same room and he was civil.

Bryn sat next to Eric. "Any news?"

"Not yet," Dad offered. "Julian's the best doctor. He'll do everything he can."

The swallow of coffee threatened to come back up. Dad had no idea what Julian Proctor was capable of. Eric leaned over, placed a kiss on Bryn's cheek—warmed to the comfort of being able to do it—and whispered, "I'm scared, Bryn."

Bryn laced her fingers in his and whispered back, "Trust God. Isn't that what you always tell me?"

He grinned. "We really do make a good team. And nothing's keeping us from staying that way."

Dad interrupted what he hoped would be a positive response from Bryn.

"You working on the morning show host's murder?"

"And the three before that. Same killer," Eric offered.

"Been talk at the club," Dad grunted.

Eric shifted. "What kind of talk? By who?"

"Everyone. I know how some gentlemen feel about women and careers. To each his own."

And tolerance continued to allow hate to breed.

"All this waiting is driving me crazy." Dad jumped up. "I'm going to… I don't know. Walk around. Go to the gift shop or something."

Eric turned to Bryn. "Do you want to finish that conversation now? I need to get my mind off the fact a crazy man has a scalpel to my mom."

"I'm not sure now is the right time. Let's wait till we can be alone. Okay?"

"Okay." Eric silently prayed for his mother.

Julian Proctor stepped into the waiting room. "Hello,

Detective Hale." He scanned the room for Dad. "Here to question me further or out of concern for your mother?"

Eric thrust himself into the doctor's face, about to blow a gasket. "If you so much as—"

"Calm down, Detective Hale." Dark eyes danced, drunk with power and amusement. "You owe me an apology, respect and a thank-you. Your mother could have died. *I* saved her."

Bryn sat in the passenger seat on the way home, reeling from the events since early afternoon. Eric's mom had made it through surgery successfully at the hands of Julian Proctor, of all people, but she was still in critical condition. Proctor told Mr. Hale it looked good and he felt she'd pull through. Her near-death experience had shaken something loose in Mr. Hale. He'd been polite the rest of the night. She only hoped it wouldn't fade if—when—Mrs. Hale recovered.

Eric hadn't pressured her to pick up where they left off, and she was thankful. Bone-tired, she grabbed her purse from the floorboard as Eric parked in her driveway. "How you holding up?"

"Decent."

"You've been through two packs of Twizzlers."

"Like I said. Decent." He grinned. "I can't believe Proctor did the surgery on my mother. If he thinks I owe him and will look the other way if he's involved—and I'm almost certain he is—then he has another think coming." Sighing he popped a Twizzler. "About earlier..."

"Eric, I'm gonna tell you everything, but after the last few hours I'm wiped out and you need to get back to your dad."

"Okay. But at least tell me you know we belong together."

Bryn pressed her hand to his cheek. Did they belong

together? How would he react if…"What if I said I didn't
want children? Would you think we belong together then?"

Eric's brow creased. "Since when?"

"I'm older. Devoted to my career." Even if it would be
from behind a desk.

"Why can't you have both? Be a mom and an agent."

Bryn's throat convulsed. "Just answer the question."

Eric worked his jaw, stared straight ahead. "I… I don't
know. You know how I feel. I haven't changed my mind.
I find it hard to believe that you have." He turned, tipped
her chin. "I don't believe you have. You're picking the one
thing you know I want most and trying to push me away.
Why?" He searched her eyes.

The one thing he wanted most. And she couldn't give
him it. The day couldn't have gotten any worse. "I'm going
to go to bed."

"You can't sleep this conversation away, but I'm not
going to press you. I am, however, going to pray."

Bryn stepped out of the SUV. "There are some things
even prayer can't change." She hurried to the front door.

He followed. "I'm not bringing it up. I just want to help
you clear the house."

"Holt's car is here. House doesn't need cleared." As if
on cue, Holt opened the front door.

"Everything cool?" he asked Bryn, then looked at Eric.
"You coming in a while?"

"No. I'm leaving." Eric's cheek twitched. He may not be
happy with the way the night was ending, but Bryn couldn't
handle any more. Not now.

Bryn stepped inside. "Everything's good." With Rusty
behind bars and Julian at the hospital, she didn't need the
extra protection, but she'd take it.

Holt gave them both a flat once-over. "I'm exhausted."
He dipped his chin in a nod to Eric and sailed into the guest
bedroom on the right, the door clicking shut behind him.

"Lock up, Bryn."

"Always do."

Silence hung, then Eric trudged down the drive to his car, leaving her alone with her thoughts.

Needing something warm to drink that wasn't full of caffeine, Bryn headed to the kitchen to make warm milk while Newton roamed the yard and did his business. After locking up and drinking her milk, she washed her face, climbed into bed and reached for the remote.

It wasn't on her bedside table.

"Okay, this is getting out of control." She jumped out of the bed and slid to the floor, searching underneath. No remote.

She checked behind the bedside table, on the TV entertainment center, the dresser and the writing desk. *Nope.*

What would she have done with that thing?

"God, am I losing my mind? Going crazy? Help me!"

She froze at the bedroom door.

"Her loopy slipups. She's had a lot of stress and it was messing with her mind..."

That's what Sandra Logan, Bridgette's best friend, had said during her interview. Bridgette had a lot on her plate. Slipups.

Racing to her computer, she booted up and entered her password, then pulled up the reports. Twenty minutes later, she had another connection.

Cat Weaver's husband said she'd been forgetful. Couldn't find students' tests. Mentioned she was going out of her mind at times. Kendra Kennick's husband said the same thing, that she'd misplaced or lost things. She'd even left her car door open all night long—but she'd been working herself to death. So had Cat Weaver since she'd taken a chair on the sociology committee and was preparing a group of interns to go to Papua New Guinea.

Annalise Hemmingway's assistant and friend said she'd

been frazzled before her death. Was dropping the ball at home and on a few cases.

They all had been stressed out. She'd been questioning her ability to do this job. Mounted on top of other things—like Ohio—it only made sense to think she was cracking up.

Could the killer have been getting inside her house, inside all the victims' homes? Was it part of the thrill for him? Had to be. But *how* was he getting inside? The doors and windows were locked. None of the victims had reported a break-in. "Think, Bryn. Think."

How would a killer get inside? It'd have to be early morning after she left for work. "If I were a killer, how would I get into this house without tipping off a trained agent?" She stood in her living room and scanned every angle. Stopped on the fireplace. She frowned. Unless he was Santa, he wasn't coming down the chimney.

But how?

She rushed through the kitchen and into the garage, flipping on the light. The corner windows. Bryn crossed the concrete floor, rounded the boxes blocking the view of the two side windows. Eric might have missed them. Out of sight, out of mind.

They slid open easily.

Unlocked.

But the door leading from the garage into the kitchen stayed locked during the day.

Down. Down? She glanced upward. *No stinking way!*

The attic drop-down door.

Trembling, she pulled the rope that opened it. She needed a ladder, but someone six feet or more, with some muscle, could easily pull himself up. Eric had done it in the steam room when he'd shimmied into the vent.

Bryn grabbed a flashlight off the wooden workbench, pulled a six-foot metal ladder over and climbed up, scrambling into the attic. It was at least ten degrees cooler, with pink insulation covering the walls, she creaked across the boards, shining the light.

She searched for signs that someone had been up here. Lying in wait.

She followed the boards to another drop-down door. Insulation was missing.

Dusty footprints.

Someone *had* been in her attic. Countless times.

She pushed the square door, and it easily dropped open into the vacant guest room closet. Good thing Holt was in the other bedroom or she might have been shot.

Bryn wasn't crazy. The killer had been messing with her. All this time. But it couldn't be Rusty alone because the candle had been left burning after they had him in custody. He'd had some help.

Julian Proctor? He was cunning. Could he have been here early in the morning and then made it to the hospital? Surgeries took place as early as five and six. He could have worked around them.

She called her analyst. "Percy, I need a favor."

"Name it."

"The hospital won't give out surgery dates for Julian Proctor. I'm going to get a subpoena, but that'll take more than a minute, so I'm about to email you a few personal dates. Once you have Proctor's surgery schedule, I want you to cross-reference the two. See if he was free of surgery on those days."

"You got it."

She hung up and went to work remembering the dates, jotting them into the email. Off the case was out the window. Her home was involved!

If Proctor wasn't in surgery on those days, he could have snuck into her house. She'd know more once she had a team out to dust for prints and analyze the shoe prints on the attic floor. Maybe she'd catch a break and discover Proctor wore the same size shoe.

She was one step closer to proving she belonged in the field. She wasn't crazy. When Bryn was done, there wouldn't be anything left of Proctor's life that hadn't been turned inside out.

Now who wasn't able to do her job?

Bryn sat in Dr. Warner's office, still waiting on Percy's findings. The dusty shoe impression had been a size eleven. Proctor, at more than six feet, could easily wear that size. Or even Rusty for that matter. But there hadn't been multiple-size shoeprints.

No fingerprints had been found in the house. She wasn't shocked. He was a meticulous man. She gripped her cell and bounced a knee. Bryn should have called Eric when she'd discovered someone had been in her home. But after he dropped her off last Friday night, hope had been severed for them on a personal level and professionally she was off the case. A new agent—Agent Reichs—was now assisting, but it didn't appear he'd conveyed the findings with Eric yet, as Eric hadn't called Bryn. Of course, it was only eight in the morning. The man probably hadn't even had a chance. It was better this way. No more direct contact between them, but it throbbed into her bones.

"You're distracted, Agent Eastman. You might want to put your phone away." Dr. Warner rested his elbows on his knees. His typical "I'm listening" gesture.

"I can't. Not today. I'm waiting on an important call." One that would confirm she was mentally capable. "I'm not going back to a desk." Her phone buzzed. "I have to take this." She answered. "Percy, what do you have?"

"I did like you asked and cross-referenced the dates and times. He was free three days, but the other four, he had surgeries and appointments."

"How many of his free days were after we arrested Rusty Beckham?"

Computer keys clacked.

"He had surgeries on all the dates after Beckham was arrested."

Bryn's excitement crashed with his words. *Now what?* "Thanks, Percy."

"Agent Eastman?" Dr. Warner's voice was quiet, calming. "You're agitated."

She hung up and paced in front of the fish tank. Someone had been messing with her mind. Messing with all their minds.

"I haven't been misplacing things after all. I'm not crazy." She folded her arms across her chest, rubbing her upper arm as she stared at the swirl of fish. "But the killer wants me to believe I am."

"Why do you say that?"

"He's been getting into my house. Through the garage and the attic. Misplacing my things. Letting Newton out." She followed a yellow-and-royal-blue fish as it nosed through the sand. "He toyed with all his victims this way."

"Why do you think he would do that?"

Torment. To make her feel incompetent. Weak. "To make us second-guess our strength. All the victims had mentioned this to friends or family. It worked. Almost worked on me." Bryn stroked the glass.

"That upsets the fish, Agent Eastman. Don't touch the glass."

Bryn dropped her finger and faced Dr. Warner. "In his mind, we infringed on a perfect society. Of men. How dare women believe that we could aspire to be more than barefoot and pregnant if that's what we wanted?"

An all-male society.

She glanced back at the tank. A shiver snaked into her bones.

Perfection.

More valuable. More beautiful.

Bryn's heart thumped against her chest. Glancing across the room, she spotted a set of golf clubs in the corner. Non-chalantly, she strode across the room as her mind raced. Dr. Warner fit the mold. He held power over her mind. A patient would trust him. Confide in him. "You play golf?" She picked up a nine iron. "Eric plays golf. I think I told you that."

"I'm fair."

She inched toward the fish tank, rolling the club with her fingers. She'd been sitting here for the past month watching his perfect world encased in glass. Her hands shook as she made her way back to the tank. The treasure chest caught her eye.

"Which golf course do you use?" She gripped the metal club.

"Several. Depends on my mood. Would you put my club back in its bag?"

"What would happen, Dr. Warner, if you put female fish into your tank? Overcrowding? Would it upset the fish? Interrupt a perfect environment?"

The killer had taken a token of jewelry as a trophy.

A treasure.

His ego would have delighted in hiding the treasures in plain sight.

Dr. Warner stood, still relaxed. But his eyes turned cold. Like Rand's at the trial when they'd made contact for one last time.

She'd played into his hand. The betrayal burned into her muscles. "Did you provide therapy for any of the victims?"

He stepped toward her. "I did. Bridgette Danforth. And Cat Weaver."

"Yet you failed to mention it." What about the other

two victims? Was he lying? *No.* A proud, arrogant smile reached his dead eyes. More evil masquerading like light.

"You didn't ask, and these sessions are about your mental health, Agent Eastman." He moved in calculating strides toward her.

"Let's stop playing games." She held his gaze as they sized each other up. She had to know. Right now. She raised the golf club and swung it with all her might into the glass.

"No!"

Water gushed, nearly toppling her over as it crashed to the floor with shards of glass. Her phone fell into the river of water, but she held fast and grabbed the treasure chest, thrusting it open to reveal a ring, bracelet, necklace and an earring.

Dr. Warner lunged, knocking her to the ground. She clawed for the golf club, but he batted it away. Heated poison laced his string of curses. "You think you're so special. Coming in here gloating about how you can beat the killer at his own game and yet here I've been sitting across from you the whole time. You're pathetic, Agent Eastman."

She twisted underneath him and broke free. Struggling to her feet, she lurched for her purse, but it was missing. He'd taken it! While she was taking a golf club—when her eyes weren't on him. No gun.

Sprinting for the door, she slipped, righted her balance and grabbed the handle, throwing the door open and bolting into the hallway for the exit.

Yanking her hair, Dr. Warner pulled her off her feet and onto the floor. A splitting pain burst from her tailbone. Her scalp stung. She raised her legs and kicked his chest, sending him across the hall and into the wall.

Jumping up, forcing herself not to think of the blinding pain, she ran for the exit door and pushed. She rammed it with her side and pushed again.

"Emergency locks. In case an unstable patient tries to run away."

"You mean victim," she spat.

"No. I meant patient." His level of calm raised hairs on her arms. She had two choices. Run for the door at the end of the hall, which probably led to the basement or try to barrel past him and make it to the front door.

The basement offered no exit.

"Who's in control now, Agent Eastman? I won't be as gracious as Scott Mulhoney. He was going to simply let you go quick and fast. I won't. The burning in your lungs will be excruciating. I won't just take what makes you a woman. I'll take your last breath. And I'll enjoy every second."

Bryn froze. Dr. Warner had ripped a new gash in her heart. Voiced out loud everything she already felt.

Scott Mulhoney had ripped away her womanhood.

Her mind blanked. She raised her arms in defense, a second too late.

Something pricked the side of her neck.

Feet like lead wouldn't move.

Darkness vacuumed up the light and fell like a heavy blanket over her heart.

Her mind.

Her eyes.

SIXTEEN

Eric stared at the phone and growled. It was Monday. She was always in early on Mondays. He wanted to go by and talk to her before meeting with the new assisting agent at ten. The way Friday night ended lodged like a doughy knot in his gut. Her odd questions and the fact they still had a conversation to finish. But Bryn wasn't in and her phone went straight to voice mail.

Eric had a chance to talk to Mom after she came out of recovery on Sunday. She hadn't even known Eric was working with Bryn on the case. Didn't even know she was back in Memphis. Dad said he'd been trying to protect her. After the heart attack, Dad had realized he couldn't protect her from everything.

Mom had understood more than Dad, but it wouldn't be simple. Or easy. But the promise to try had filled Eric with fresh hope.

In order to make the whole lifetime thing a reality, he'd need Bryn to get on board, though, and she had been far from him Friday night. Not wanting kids. Pushing him away on purpose.

Not showing up this morning.

And that's why he was pulling into her driveway.

No car.

His nerves were frayed. Where was she?

Could she be at the therapist? Talking about him. About her newfound idea not to have children.

Wait.

Bryn had touched her abdomen when she told Eric she'd been shot. Couldn't stick around to hear Angela talk about the baby at Sonic.

Then the change of heart about having kids. Throwing it out there. Testing him.

He'd failed. Utterly failed. Said the wrong thing.

Thumping his fist to his brow, he groaned.

"I don't know...the one thing I want most..." Words that built a wall between them.

No. His heart splintered into pieces, sucking the breath from him and bringing unwanted moisture to his eyes. Not for him. For her. For everything she'd lost.

Stupid! He'd made jokes about Eric and Erica Hales running around. Wanting dozens of children. Bryn had pushed him away to give him some sort of freedom to find love with someone who could provide him children.

Did she not realize there was no other woman in the entire world for him? That he couldn't love anyone more? Babies or no babies. Foster or adopted. Didn't matter.

The minute she walked through the door, whether home or the office, he was going to tell her. And if he had to strap her to a chair until she believed him, he wasn't above it.

God, help her believe the truth.

His phone rang.

Bryn's analyst.

"Hey, Percy."

"Detective. Is Agent Eastman with you?"

"No. I've been looking for her myself. You have news?" Eric snagged a Twizzler, poked it in his mouth and tossed it aside.

"Well, she asked for Julian Proctor's surgical schedule. Dates and times."

"Why?"

"She thought he was the one sneaking into her house and rearranging things. He wasn't, but I went to call her back about something I did find. She's still not answering."

She wasn't crazy at all. Someone had been sneaking in and she'd discovered it. *How?* "Did she say how he was getting into her house?"

"No."

Eric had personally checked the door and windows. He paused. Garage windows. He peered inside. Noticed the attic door. Why hadn't he thought of that?

"She said the victims had all been stressed and forgetful. So I thought, what do people do when they're stressed and feeling mentally incapable? They get therapy."

Eric snorted. "Yeah, they do." Including Bryn. He jimmied the window. It was definitely locked now. He put some muscle into the old window. Nothing.

"Well, I found something."

"What's that?"

"Bridgette Danforth and Cat Weaver both extracted the same amount of cash from private accounts each week. Every Tuesday to be exact."

"How much?"

"Four hundred bucks."

"But nothing on Annalise Hemingway or Kendra Kennick?"

"Well, not Kendra exactly. But her husband also took the same amount of cash out of a private bank account. Every Thursday. Clearly, they didn't want anyone to know they were seeing a therapist. It's private, you know."

Oh yeah. Bryn had kept it hidden. "Give me Kennick's number. I'm not where I can get to my notes."

Percy rattled off Kyle Kennick's phone number and Eric called.

"Mr. Kennick. It's Detective Hale. I'd like to ask you a personal question. It may help me find your wife's murderer."

"Sure, Detective. Whatever you want." His weary voice reached across the line.

"You took out four hundred dollars a week every week. Can you tell me why?"

Silence hung on the line, then a heavy sigh filled the connection. "I didn't tell Kendra, but I was seeing a therapist. We were juggling hectic work schedules—she refused to quit her job—parenting, and a marriage which was suffering. I was overwhelmed."

"Who did you see?"

"Dr. Elliot Warner. Downtown."

Downtown. Eric's stomach bottomed out. "What was his advice?"

"In a roundabout way, he implied Kendra was choking the life out of me and to leave. I didn't, though."

Eric's temple thumped. "Thanks." He hung up and called Percy. "Get me everything you have on Dr. Elliot Warner. I need to know if he's contracted by the FBI. Include his home and work address and any other physical addresses."

Fingers racing over a keyboard sounded. "Yes, he's the FBI therapist." He rattled off his addresses.

If she wasn't at the office or home, she was probably with the killer. And she didn't even know it. Eric hit the lights and headed for the interstate.

Whatever it took to get to her.

Wet cold jolted Bryn awake, head pounding, lying on concrete. Forcing her eyes open, she surveyed her surroundings.

Water gushed from eight metal spigots at the bottom of

her enclosure. She rose from the floor, touching the small area behind her ear where Dr. Warner had injected something to knock her out.

Octagonal plexiglass housed her. About eight feet tall, five feet wide.

Like a monstrous...*fish tank*.

No escape.

Water covered her ankle deep and steadily rose.

Trapped. Like a fish.

Dr. Warner sat in a recliner, kicked back, feet propped up as if he were watching a football game. He wore a headset and a wild gleam in his eyes. "You said you wanted to jump into a tank and swim. Now's your chance."

His echoing voice filtered through the tank. Must be some kind of waterproof speakers embedded. With a thundering heart and blood rushing in her ears, Bryn pressed against the walls, groping for an escape. Nothing but thick, chilled glass.

This was how he did it. In the basement of his practice, he'd forced his victims into the tank and watched as they died in a watery grave.

Her pulse spiked as the water rushed midcalf. How long did she have before she was submerged?

Panic clawed its way through her body.

No. Stay calm. Find a way out. "How'd you get them in here?" She pounded out of fear, frustration and the need to do something, anything. That's when she realized her ring on her right finger—the amethyst—was missing. Slamming her hand against the tank, she screamed, "You won't get away with this."

"Don't touch the glass, Agent Eastman. You're upsetting me." He smirked. She skidded a glance to a table against the wall. Bags and bags of fish.

Dr. Warner followed her gaze and chuckled. "I saved them. Fish are rather resilient. Let's see if you are."

She dropped to her knees, the icy water riding up to her chest. She fumbled with the spigots, trying to cork them with her fingers. Jumping up, she flew to each side of the tank banging. "Someone will find me."

"Who? You've kept your visits a secret. Like most patients."

"Tell me how you did it." The ME hadn't found any pinpricks on their necks. She played on his ego. "You must have been slick for Bridgette Danforth to get into your car. To get them all."

"Who said I got them in my car? Who's to say I didn't have them meet me here, then I drove their cars back to familiar sites? Who's to say I didn't touch a thing but the steering wheel. Ms. Kennick's drive to her work was excruciating. I have long legs."

"When I get out of here, I'm going to wipe that smug grin off your face. Count on it."

But she'd have to beat through about four inches of plexiglass to do it. Dr. Warner was right. No one knew she was here. She had no way out.

God, help me out of this tank! Save me! Did You save me in Ohio, only to let me die like this?

"You'll do just what they did, when you realize you're helpless. Hopeless. You'll scream. Beg and acknowledge that I decide if you live or die." He inched closer and held her gaze. "How does it feel to know I own your last breath?"

No, he did not.

Anger burned in her gut. White-hot. Searing.

"You're not God."

"I don't see any God here, Agent Eastman, except me."

When you pass through the waters, I will be with you. And through the rivers, they shall not overflow you...

Neither did Bryn, but she believed, felt God's presence as scripture came to mind. And never did she need it more.

Warner might take her life. But he didn't own her soul. He wasn't about to get his sadistic satisfaction.

"I will never scream. I will not beg. And you won't win."

Fury flashed in Warner's eyes. "You will. Your body will fight for life whether you want it to or not. Proven fact. I'm going to watch you fight and fail."

Water had reached her abdomen. She let out a breath. *Breathe. Relax.*

Holt had been right. Time was too short not to spend it with the one you loved. Eric was smart. Maybe he'd figure it out, but it wouldn't be in time. Eight minutes was all she could handle underwater. With no extra oxygen and practice rusty, Bryn might only have about five.

Five minutes felt like five seconds.

Breathe.

She inhaled. Exhaled. Deep cleansing breaths, expanding her lungs.

Closing her eyes, she concentrated.

"Ask me for your life, Agent Eastman."

She stood her ground in the middle of the tank, kept her eyes closed and ignored him.

"Beg me! I own you." He smacked the glass with his hands. He was no longer in control. The instability in his voice confirmed it.

Water reached her neck, and she continued to breathe.

She ticked the seconds by in her head and prayed.

Ice water filled to her chin, and took her balance. She opened her eyes, inhaled one long breath and treaded water as it covered her head. No way out.

A minute passed.

Bryn forced herself to remain calm. Not think about five minutes from now.

Dr. Warner was losing his resolve. He paced and cursed as she calmly treaded water, reserving her energy. Enraged, he grabbed at his hair. Bryn wasn't obeying. Wasn't dying a torturous death.

He would not win. He would not.

Three minutes ticked by. She kept her focus on him. He banged on the glass and she jerked but kept her breath.

Four minutes.

Her brain reminded her body she needed oxygen, and her lungs burned; a burst of anxiety rippled in her chest. She hung on.

Fake it.

Could she fake drowning? If she gave him what he wanted, he might drain the tank, giving her time to breathe. And to fight.

But it might not work.

Through the waters.

Now or never.

She jerked in the water, widening her eyes and giving the illusion of panic.

Dr. Warner paused. His eyes danced with anticipation of her demise. He laughed and clapped his hands, inching closer to the glass. "I told you. You can't help it, can you?"

She drove her body to the top of the tank, banging and writhing.

"You're going to die, Agent Eastman."

Lungs flaming, she released a few bubbles and let the water turn her body over, facing the floor of the tank, limp. Lifeless. She jerked once. Twice. Then relaxed.

Dr. Warner's maniacal laughter grated her skin, but she didn't dare move.

Seven minutes.

Eight.

Can't. Hold. On.

Eric...

* * *

Weaving in and out of traffic, Eric crushed his foot to the gas pedal. His phone rang, and he put Percy on speaker. "What else do you have, Percy?"

"Dr. Warner's originally from Florida. Came from an abusive home. Until his father beat his mother to death and shot himself. Warner went into foster care after that. You know what the foster system can be like. He was passed around due to violent behavior. One family said he was cruel to their daughters. Broke their toys, frightened them while they slept, hid their clothes and games. They sent him back into the system. It escalated at fifteen with his last foster family."

Eric gritted his teeth. "What'd he do?"

"Parents couldn't prove it, but their four-year-old daughter nearly drowned in the pool. She told her parents Warner tossed her into the deep end and wouldn't get her out. Knew she couldn't swim. He didn't deny it, but didn't admit it, either. They put him back in the system until he turned eighteen."

"Who saved the girl?"

"A girl who lived next door. Said Warner was just standing there watching."

A girl rescuing one of his first victims. That would infuriate him. His hatred of women would have increased. Instead of despising his abusive father, he placed blame on his mother. He would have wanted her to fight for herself, and him, but instead she would have been too weak. Who knew what Elliot Warner had witnessed in that home, under the hands of a madman father?

"Anything after that?"

"Can't connect it exactly, but a psychology professor went missing from Florida State, after giving an internship to a female student instead of Warner. But, again, nothing could be proved, and they never found the body."

Eric's stomach roiled and burned. "Please tell me that's all."

"He's a member of Edgewood Golf Club."

It could have been Warner who'd locked them in the steam room. Not Proctor. If he'd been there at the time. "Can you send me a picture of this guy?"

"You got it."

His phone chimed, and he glanced over.

Acid shot into his throat.

The guy sitting with Julian at the golf club. The man who'd left the table. Eric had the wrong guy, and Warner knew it. Let him sit there and interrogate Proctor.

He'd been right under his nose!

Eric banged the steering wheel and parked on the street, then shot across the sidewalk to Warner's office building. He climbed the steps and turned the knob.

Locked.

Why would he lock the doors if he was seeing patients?

The thought of something horrible happening to Bryn sent his elbow to the window, breaking the glass. He climbed inside, tearing the leather sleeve of his jacket.

Inside, he pulled his weapon and crept across the foyer and down the hall. Water spilled out onto the hardwood. He pushed open the door. Glass covered the floor; tables and chairs had been knocked over.

Bryn's purse lay on the desk.

He called in backup, hung up and moved through the halls to a door that led down a set of stairs into a dank basement. Eric tiptoed down each stair until it opened up into a large room.

God, please let Bryn be okay. Keep her safe. Help me.

Sweat snaked down temples and back. His heartbeat pulsed in his ears.

A huge tank, like an oversize drum cage, with a thick glass door swung open wide met him, water spilling across the concrete floor.

Inside the tank, Bryn lay limp. Hair sprawled across her face.

No!

His legs turned shaky and his chest constricted, but he rushed across the floor, stepped into the tank, and knelt in front of her. "Bryn! Bryn," he whispered.

She didn't move.

How could he have lost her when he hadn't had the chance to make her his yet?

His face flushed, then turned cold.

Checking her pulse, he willed his own heart to slow down.

There it was! So faint he almost believed he was imagining it.

Scuffling from the other side of the room drew his attention.

Eric jumped to his feet, pointed his weapon and waited for Dr. Warner to come out into the open. He wanted to shoot first, ask questions later.

Were those sirens in the distance?

Elliot Warner stepped into the room.

"Hands over your head. Slow."

"Ah, Detective Hale. You're a tad late." He chuckled but didn't resist arrest as Eric read him his rights.

He thought she was dead. No wonder he didn't bother to fight. He knew it was over. He must be relishing in destroying what he'd think of as his greatest threat. A female law enforcer.

But she wasn't dead. *Hurry up, first responders!* Eric had no idea how long she'd been under—how much damage had been done. He itched to go to her. To hold her.

The quiet echo of sirens now screeched.

"You might like to know, she was brave at first. But in the end, she panicked. Like they all do."

Eric balled his fists and reined in his temper.

Reinforcements barreled into the basement and hauled Warner away.

Racing to Bryn, he turned her over, brushed her hair from her face. "You brave woman, I love you," he murmured. His hand trembled against her pale cheek; her lips were tinged blue.

Thank you, God. For saving her.

He brushed his lips across Bryn's forehead, and her eyes flickered open.

"Eric," she rasped and coughed. "You are a Jedi."

He kissed her hand and chuckled. "About time you admit it." It was about time she admitted she loved him and wanted to spend her life with him, too.

Paramedics entered, and he backed away as they checked Bryn's vitals. Her body shook, and her bottom lip quivered.

"You scared me half to death." He brushed a finger down her cheek. "He must have thought you were dead."

"That was the idea." Bryn coughed and shoved an oxygen mask away.

"Held your breath?"

"Beat my old time. Nine minutes and some odd seconds." She coughed again and sputtered. "I'm so glad this is over." Relief washed a hint of color into her cheeks.

He kissed her nose. "I was terrified I wouldn't make it in time."

"I'm alive. Thank God."

So good to hear her thanking God, acknowledging Him again. Eric smiled. "That you are. Warner thinks you're dead."

Bryn stood tall. "Let's go show him I'm not."

SEVENTEEN

Bryn watched on the monitor as Eric questioned Elliot Warner. Thinking he'd landed the big fish, he cooperated and told Eric everything he wanted to know—against his attorney's wishes. And she thought that only happened in the movies.

Warner played racquetball with a friend of Annalise Hemingway's husband. After hearing how she shredded men, he met her at a society event, telling her about a fake client who was being abused by her husband and was too scared to talk to a lawyer. He then invited her to come to that fake client's session to coax her into leaving and divorcing him.

Annalise called him on the breach of confidence, even though he'd never given a name, but her heart was especially tender to abused women since she'd been abused by her first husband. Warner took great pride in that. Knowing exactly where to strike emotionally.

He admitted to smothering the women until they passed out, then putting them into the tank, after removing a token for his treasure chest.

"How'd you take Kendra Kennick?"

"She was eager to keep her clients' unsavory behavior quiet, so I told her I had information on one. Which I did. John Linden had been shacking up with a hooker. Heard that at the club, but what do I care? She was a means to a desire. But Kendra thought I cared. She came to see me."

Angela.

Eric rubbed his temple. "What about Rusty Beckham?"

"What about him? I have nothing to do with the man who took a swing at Agent Eastman."

Eric was covering extra bases, just in case Rusty had lied. After days in jail, Rusty realized he might go down for four murders he hadn't committed, and he'd confessed to the attacks on Bryn, except the steam room. He'd done it in honor of Julian Proctor. The guy was a sicko. So was Julian, but he hadn't been involved in any of this, and he was going to walk away and continue to breed hate.

There were hundreds of Rusty Beckhams out there just waiting to hurt women in the name of Julian Proctor and his disgusting coalition.

"I am glad he didn't follow through on his threat. My most satisfying one yet." Dr. Warner's dead eyes filled with dark amusement.

Eric bristled.

"Oh, don't get upset, Detective Hale. You'll get all the credit for uncovering the killer. Doesn't that feel good? Besides, she could never give you what you want."

He was going to tell Eric. Bryn wanted to be the one to tell him, to let him decide.

"Dr. Warner, I'm going to need you to write all of this down exactly as you've told it to me."

"Don't you want to know what she couldn't give you?"

Bryn couldn't bust in there and stop him. Eric needed that handwritten confession. She gnawed her thumbnail and tapped her foot on the floor.

"I'll tell you what. You write your confession, and I'll be happy to hear everything you and Bryn talked about."

Dr. Warner squinted, then grinned. "You already know, don't you?"

"Write."

He chuckled. "You do." He scribbled across the notepad. How could he know? Dr. Warner finished, signed it and slid it across the table. "Would you like to know anything else she said about you?"

Eric glanced at the camera and winked. "How about I let her tell me?"

"From the grave?"

Bryn stepped out of the video room and inhaled. This man had no power over her. She turned the knob and opened the door to the interrogation room.

Dr. Warner's face was priceless. Eyes bulging, fear, fury.

"Did you know, Dr. Warner, that Bryn held the record at Rhodes College for holding her breath a solid eight minutes?"

Bryn stalked across the room and stood beside Eric. "Like I said before. You don't own me. You're not the only one who can mess with minds. All it took was a second for you to see me panic and fake a death before you drained the tank. Predictable." She took the notepad from Eric. "Thanks for this." She made it halfway across the room and stopped. "They weren't sure what to do with all your fish you saved and secured in your plastic bags."

"Those are my fish!" A stream of expletives shot from his mouth. He tried to rise, but Eric pinned him down.

"No. They're mine now. When I sit on my couch and watch them swim, I'll think of you. I'll think of how I came in like a pirate and stole all your treasure." She opened the door. "And I'll smile."

She quietly closed it behind her.

Eric wrapped up the case reports while Bryn handled paperwork on her end. She'd had to stand at the monitor and be reminded of all the things she couldn't give him. All the things she could give probably never crossed his mind.

It was time to finish the discussion. He wasn't taking no for answer. He found her taking down the photos and wiping down the whiteboards they'd used in the major case room.

"I wrapped up my end."

She turned and smiled. "I'm almost done. Other than notifying the victims' loved ones that we caught the monster." The glow in Bryn's eyes, now that she'd been approved for permanent field duty, put a major grin in Eric's heart.

He leaned against the door, crossed one ankle over the other. "I liked the pirate analogy. All it was missing was an 'aaargh' and a quip about walking the plank."

Bryn snorted and put the lid on the case file box.

"I didn't know you took his fish."

"I didn't." She laughed. "They're floating in tanks at Petco as we speak. I don't have room for a tank that big in my house, and it's not a permanent place anyway."

"Clever girl."

"I try." She caught his gaze and held it. "We did it."

"We did. We make a great team." Clasping her hand, he brought it to his chest. "I love you. I've always loved you." He pressed her hand to his lips. "I will always love you."

Her hand trembled beneath his. "I—"

Shutting down her protest with his index finger to her lips, he grinned. "You are the bravest woman I've ever met. You've endured more than any one person should ever have to. If I could wipe all that pain away, I would. But it's made you who you are. Compassionate. Passionate. Kind. Strong. So strong. And it brought you back to me." He pulled her to him. "You can't tell me you don't love me. I know you do."

Tears filled her eyes. "Dr. Warner was right. I didn't tell you everything. I wish things were different but…"

"Are you talking about what happened when Scott Mulhoney shot you?"

Bryn gasped. "You do know. How?"

He cupped her face. "I figured it out. Bryn, I love you. I want to be with you. Kids. No kids. You're not taking anything from me. Unless you refuse to be with me. Then you're taking everything away."

A tear slid down her cheek. "You might resent me."

"I could never resent you." He pressed his lips to her ear. "I adore you."

"He robbed me of being a woman." A hiccup escaped her mouth.

"No, love. He didn't. He didn't even rob you of being a mom." He brushed a kiss to her lips. "We can adopt. We can be foster parents. Both. We can buy an orphanage." He laughed. "Whatever you want. Whenever you want. I just need you."

She searched his eyes, and he prayed she'd see he was telling the absolute truth.

"Adoption would be enough for you?"

"Bryn, *you* are enough for me." He kissed her knuckles. "Who knows what God will bless us with?"

"I do love you."

"That's what I've been waiting to hear." Tenderly he drew her to him, kissing her with every ounce of passion, letting it build and soar. Tugging her closer, he slid his hands into her hair and explored the wonderfulness that was all Bryn. Like they were made for each other, she melded into him and matched his fervor.

Finally, she broke the kiss. "If I could choose how to lose my last breath, it'd be kissing you."

"Marry me and we'll have a lifetime of kisses." His heart hammered in his chest.

"Yes." Her grin sent him flying. "Now kiss me breathless."

He pecked her nose. "You do realize that sounded more morbid than romantic, right?"

Bryn giggled. "Shut up and kiss me crazy, Hale."

"Now that sounded like true love."

He claimed her lips in awe that Bryn Eastman finally belonged to him.

EPILOGUE

Ten months later

Newton jumped up and put his paws on the kitchen counter. "What did I tell you about that, you big ball of fur?" Bryn nudged him off the counter, placed the casserole Piper had brought over on the counter and grinned at Eric. Watching him rock Abigail always sent butterflies into her stomach.

At four months old, she was growing as plump as Newton. With dark hair and eyes, she looked just like her daddy, even if they hadn't conceived her. She was theirs. Heart and soul.

"You're spoiling her. You should put her in the cradle if she's asleep," Bryn said. She was just as bad. Abigail would only be a baby for so long. She wanted every moment.

"Angela called. She's settled in Texas. Got a job working as a secretary at a paper company. She sounded happy."

"Is she going to take those night classes?" Bryn asked as she scooped Abigail into her arms and pressed a kiss to her rosy little lips, then laid her in the cradle and took her daughter's place in Eric's lap. Wrapping her arms around him, she nuzzled into his neck. "You smell good."

"I smell like spit-up."

She giggled against his collarbone. "Holt's not coming to dinner. He's going undercover for a while. The Mexican cartel he's been investigating might have had something to do with that missing DEA agent."

"If anyone can get in and ferret out the truth, it's Holt. We'll pray for him."

"Already started."

Eric stole a kiss, giving her goose bumps. Bryn believed he'd always do that. They'd had a small ceremony in Hawaii. Eric's parents had flown in her parents, as well as Luke, Piper and Holt. Then after two weeks of wedded bliss, they'd come home to the house Eric had purchased years ago. The house he'd always meant to live out his days with Bryn in.

Five months later, they'd experienced the birth of their daughter, named after Eric's sister, Abby. Bryn had been inside the delivery room with Angela while Eric had paced the waiting area like a madman—at least that's how Luke had described it.

Angela had moved to Texas with Tamika to start fresh. And Bryn and Eric had a little bundle of joy all their own. He was such a wonderful dad and husband.

"Whacha thinking, babe?"

She pecked his lips. "How much I love you."

"I love you more."

"I don't think so."

Eric cocked an eyebrow. "How many sirens have you switched on to get to me?"

"Please don't ever make me do that." She toyed with his hair.

God had blessed her in so many ways. Looking back, God had been by her side. Never left. Through pain and tragedy, a place of intimacy with her Savior had been born.

She closed her eyes and thanked God for bringing her here.

Back to Eric.
To Abigail.
To a place of healing.
A place of hope.
And her heart couldn't be fuller.

* * * * *

Dear Reader,

There's a saying that when it rains it pours. Bryn experienced a lot of tragedy in her life, which shattered her dreams, family and hope. She felt as if she couldn't trust God anymore because He forgot about her. Maybe you've felt the same way. It took a while, but Bryn finally saw that even with all the horrible things that had happened to her, God loved her. He never stopped. He was still faithful and in control. If it hadn't been for those very tragedies, Bryn never would have gone into law enforcement. It was there she discovered her passion to help others. She felt more satisfied than ever before. And it was the terrible gunshot wound that brought her back to Memphis where she and Eric rekindled their love. If we let God, He'll take all those tragedies, all the rain that's been pouring, and make something beautiful grow from it. All things really do work together for good to those who love God. Even the pain. God showed Bryn He had a good plan for her life that was full of hope. He has a good plan full of hope for yours, as well.

I'd love for you to get *Patched In*! My newsletter subscribers receive first looks at book covers, excerpts and occasional *free* novellas, as well as notifications when new books release. Sign up today at www.jessicarpatch. com. Please feel free to email me at jessica@jessicarpatch. com, join me on my Facebook page, www.facebook.com/ jessicarpatch for daily discussions and take a peek at my Pinterest board (pinterest.com/jessicarpatch) to meet the characters and get an up-close view of the scenes from the book.

Warmly,
Jessica

REQUEST YOUR FREE BOOKS!

2 FREE RIVETING INSPIRATIONAL NOVELS
PLUS 2 FREE MYSTERY GIFTS

Love Inspired®
SUSPENSE
RIVETING INSPIRATIONAL ROMANCE

YES! Please send me 2 FREE Love Inspired® Suspense novels and my 2 FREE mystery gifts (gifts are worth about $10). After receiving them, if I don't wish to receive any more books, I can return the shipping statement marked "cancel." If I don't cancel, I will receive 4 brand-new novels every month and be billed just $4.99 per book in the U.S. or $5.49 per book in Canada. That's a savings of at least 17% off the cover price. It's quite a bargain! Shipping and handling is just 50¢ per book in the U.S. and 75¢ per book in Canada.* I understand that accepting the 2 free books and gifts places me under no obligation to buy anything. I can always return a shipment and cancel at any time. Even if I never buy another book, the two free books and gifts are mine to keep forever.

123/323 IDN GH5Z

Name	(PLEASE PRINT)	
Address		Apt. #
City	State/Prov.	Zip/Postal Code

Signature (if under 18, a parent or guardian must sign)

Mail to the **Reader Service**:
IN U.S.A.: P.O. Box 1867, Buffalo, NY 14240-1867
IN CANADA: P.O. Box 609, Fort Erie, Ontario L2A 5X3

**Are you a current subscriber to Love Inspired® Suspense books
and want to receive the larger-print edition?
Call 1-800-873-8635 or visit www.ReaderService.com.**

* Terms and prices subject to change without notice. Prices do not include applicable taxes. Sales tax applicable in N.Y. Canadian residents will be charged applicable taxes. Offer not valid in Quebec. This offer is limited to one order per household. Not valid for current subscribers to Love Inspired Suspense books. All orders subject to credit approval. Credit or debit balances in a customer's account(s) may be offset by any other outstanding balance owed by or to the customer. Please allow 4 to 6 weeks for delivery. Offer available while quantities last.

Your Privacy—The Reader Service is committed to protecting your privacy. Our Privacy Policy is available online at www.ReaderService.com or upon request from the Reader Service.

We make a portion of our mailing list available to reputable third parties that offer products we believe may interest you. If you prefer that we not exchange your name with third parties, or if you wish to clarify or modify your communication preferences, please visit us at www.ReaderService.com/consumerchoice or write to us at Reader Service Preference Service, P.O. Box 9062, Buffalo, NY 14240-9062. Include your complete name and address.

*A rookie K-9 officer must work together with her former
love to stay alive and solve the mystery of his sister's
murder.*

*Read on for an excerpt from
HONOR AND DEFEND,
the next book in the exciting K-9 cop miniseries
ROOKIE K-9 UNIT.*

K-9 police officer Ellen Foxcroft shot a sideways glance at
the man who drove in silent concentration. Just ten minutes
ago, they'd picked up three puppies from Sophie Williams.
Not only was she a trainer for the Desert Valley K-9 training
center, she also worked with the Prison Pups program. A
program Lee Earnshaw, the man behind the wheel, was
intimately familiar with since he'd worked with the program
up until two weeks ago, when he'd been released from
prison. Framed. Set up by a dirty cop, he'd lost two years
of his life.

"I appreciate you giving me this chance to work with you
and the pups. Not everyone believes I'm innocent in spite
of the press conference and Ken Bucks's arrest," Lee said.

"You're welcome."

"I just really want to put it all behind me."

"I'm sure you do." Probably easier said than done.
This was Lee's second day on the job. Two days ago, after
much self-examination and encouragement from Sophie,
she'd approached Lee about working for her and he'd been
reluctant. With their history, she couldn't say she blamed

him. They'd dated in high school. Until she'd allowed her mother to chase him away. Her jaw tightened. She didn't want to go there.

Instead, she remembered the flare of attraction she'd felt just from being in his presence again. Just from talking to him and looking into his eyes. Eyes she'd never been able to forget.

She couldn't help studying his features. Brown hair with a brand-new cut, brown eyes that at times looked hard and cold but were always alive and warm when he worked with the animals. His strong jaw held a five-o'clock shadow.

"I can understand your frustrations, Lee. I feel the same way—"

The back windshield shattered and Ellen gave a low scream of surprise. Lee jerked the wheel to the right. "Get down!" Outside sounds rushed through the missing window. Someone was shooting at them!

Don't miss HONOR AND DEFEND
by Lynette Eason, available wherever
Love Inspired® Suspense books and ebooks are sold.

www.LoveInspired.com

Reading Has Its Rewards

Earn **FREE BOOKS!**

Register at **Harlequin My Rewards** and submit your Harlequin purchases from wherever you shop to earn points for free books and other exclusive rewards.

Plus submit your purchases from now till May 30th for a chance to win a $500 Visa Card*.

Visit **HarlequinMyRewards.com** today

MYR16R1